T

ASSASSINATION PLAYERS

Bailiff Mountsorrel Mysteries
Book Two

David Field

SAPERE
BOOKS

THE
ASSASSINATION
PLAYERS

Published by Sapere Books.

24 Trafalgar Road, Ilkley, LS29 8HH,
United Kingdom

saperebooks.com

ISBN: 978-0-85495-249-6

PROLOGUE

Nottingham, 1591

The distant dust cloud on the country road just north of the village of Costock warned of the approach of the retinue accompanying Justice Mortley on his journey north from Leicester to the Nottingham Assizes that were due to open on the following Monday. From the hillock to the south that overlooked the narrow, wooded defile through which the coach and its escort would travel, a man dressed in wild animal skins waved, and his companions set to work.

A massive oak tree had already been sawn almost completely through just a few feet from its base, and half a dozen brawny hands joined in the grunting effort to push it down onto the track. It landed with a shuddering thump in a cloud of dust. A quarter of a mile to the south, the leading horsemen, heavily armed and dressed in Tudor livery, heard the crash and saw the dust. They called back to the outriders on either side of the coach, and they in turn alerted their colleagues to the rear. The procession drew to a halt when the obstruction came into full view.

The felled oak blocked further progress, and one of the two lead riders dismounted with muttered oaths just as the lordly dignitary they were escorting stuck his head through the coach window and demanded to know why they had stopped. The Captain of the Guard who commanded the escort was about to explain to his lordship that a mighty fallen tree was blocking their path, when there came the sound of tortured, tearing timber, and another giant of the forest bounced down into the roadway a few yards behind them.

Sensing a trap, the captain yelled for his men to draw their weapons, just as the first crossbow bolt thudded into his throat above the top line of his cuirass. As he slid from his saddle, further bolts found their mark, and the one remaining royal man at arms was felled from behind by a massive slash from a broadsword, which took his head from his shoulders in a spray of blood.

Justice Mortley ducked hurriedly back inside the coach. He quivered in a corner until the door was roughly opened and he was dragged out into the dust, where hasty sword blades put a bloody end to his judicial career. Then with shouts of triumph and a few thankful Latin praises to God, the merciless slaughterers reclaimed the horses they had hidden further back in the trees and rode hard in the direction of distant Nottingham, leaving carrion birds to dine on the still steaming leftovers.

1

Edward Mountsorrel gazed out over the garden beds on the north side of his temporary home in Thurland Hall, whose proprietor Sir John Holles was also his employer. Sir John was the High Sheriff of Nottinghamshire and Edward was his bailiff. The apartments on the ground floor of the north wing that Edward shared with his bride of several months, the beautiful former lady's maid Elizabeth, came with the office that Edward occupied. This convenient arrangement would continue until the happy couple had saved enough to move into their own house on the vacant plot of land in Whitefriars Lane that Edward had recently purchased. It sat across the lane from where he had formerly resided with his friend and town contemporary Francis Barton, Bailiff to the Sheriff of Nottingham.

Elizabeth came up behind him and held him in her arms. 'Come back to bed, my sweet, and let us celebrate this season of new birth with loving actions that may result in a child of our own.'

Edward smiled as he turned to embrace her, kissed her on the lips, then gently shook his head. 'I cannot disobey a summons from my master, and the message was delivered some time since. I delayed only to partake of some bread and cheese, and of course to kiss you farewell.'

'You are not summoned beyond the far side of the courtyard, surely?' she said with a frown. 'Why do you bid me "farewell", as if you were bound on some journey?'

'Who can tell, given the nature of my duties?' Edward replied. 'It is not the sheriff's custom to summon me when I have barely risen from my bed, so I foresee that it must be a matter of some gravity. And since the territory over which I exercise my authority in his name does not begin until the town boundary ends, *any* call to duty requires that I take to my horse, be it for even a small distance. And so I leave you to give instruction to Meg.'

Leaving his wife to issue orders to their house girl, Edward strode through the rear door that gave access to the stables and checked that his horse had been fed, watered and rubbed down for the day, and could therefore be saddled without delay if required. Then he walked swiftly across the courtyard to the southern, and more prestigious, wing of the grand house and announced his arrival to the hall steward. He was asked to wait in the morning room, where a roaring fire was already crackling merrily, despite the prospect of another unseasonably warm spring day.

Sheriff Holles strode in with urgency written across his black-bearded face and lost no time in coming to the point.

'I trust that you have broken your fast, since I wish you to lose no time in riding south of here, to the village of Costock. There has been a terrible outrage there, two days past.'

'The nature of it?' Edward enquired, catching the mood.

Holles's eyes widened as he gave Edward the appalling tidings. 'A band of vagabonds set about the coach carrying the queen's justice north from Leicester. All the armed men who accompanied it were slaughtered, along with Justice Mortley himself. We shall have to adjourn the assize for several days, but more to the point we must catch these blackguards without delay and bring them to justice.'

The news was serious for more than one reason. The more obvious one was the effrontery to the established order, and the bloody message to the entire nation that Nottinghamshire was not a county whose roads were safe to travel. As its sheriff, Holles would no doubt be held to account in London for the fact that one of the royal justices had been brutally done to death in the county where he had the duty of preserving the Queen's Peace. Some royal official would be despatched north without delay to demand an explanation, and enquire as to what steps were being taken to identify and incarcerate those responsible.

The secondary consideration was the immediate impact that the death of Justice Mortley was likely to have on the smooth disposal of criminal justice in the county. The duties of the sheriff included presenting serious offenders, whose transgressions were too serious to be dealt with by magistrates or in Quarter Sessions, to the Assize Courts that were conducted twice yearly in the Shire Hall, where a local jury would sit in judgment under the experienced eye of a royal justice. The murder of the judge who was on his way to conduct those proceedings would delay the hearings of the five cases, which had been expected to result in hangings.

'The assize will only be delayed for a matter of days?' Edward asked as the implications sank in. 'But surely, with no royal justice…'

Holles waved his hand impatiently. 'Word has been sent to Justice Brigham in Derby, who has recently completed his list. He would have ended his circuit there, but now must travel east to take the assize that was allocated to Justice Mortley. But that is not my immediate concern. Find those responsible for this treasonous act and bring them back here to be hanged, disembowelled and quartered in due course at Tyburn, with their heads impaled on London Bridge!'

Edward had never seen his employer so overcome by the enormity of a crime, although it was only a matter of weeks since Holles had been appointed for a year's term of office. But Holles had good reason, apart from the prospect of the imminent arrival of interrogators from the royal court. The slaughter of a justice was a strident challenge to law and order in the realm, little short of a treasonous attempt on the queen's life, and it had to be met with immediate counteraction. As the sheriff's bailiff, it was Edward's duty to bring offenders of all description to justice, and the more heinous the crime, the greater the need for swift action. After assuring Holles that he would leave no stone unturned in his efforts to identify and manacle those responsible, he turned to leave.

Holles called him back. 'Employ the utmost caution for your *own* safety, Edward. These are desperate men whose true purpose and mission we cannot at this stage determine. Take constables with you, and ensure that you are adequately armed. This latest news is grave enough, without my losing a valued bailiff and having to comfort a grieving widow who is not yet three months married.'

Despite the wise warning, Edward opted to ride south alone. For one thing, he would lose valuable time in gathering enough constables to constitute a meaningful force. Furthermore, the sudden appearance of another armed contingent in a previously sleepy village, so soon after the bloody outrage that it had recently witnessed, would quiet certain tongues that he needed to keep loosened. As a former country dweller himself, Edward knew only too well how quickly the veil of silence could descend upon those in an isolated community in fear of their lives.

As he clattered over Hethbeth Bridge, he reflected that there was also much truth in his master's reference to possible impending widowhood for Elizabeth, were he to ride into Costock brandishing a sword high in the air and challenging all comers in the queen's name. He watched the outlying cottages to the south of the town become less frequent in number as the cornfields and vegetable strips took over, and the only signs of life were the scrawny cows chewing the new grass of the year.

Once in Costock, Edward tied his horse to the post outside the village inn, The Plough, and went in search of its landlord. Richard Bluntstone seemed relieved enough to see him once he'd disclosed his identity, and he handed Edward a pot of the local ale. 'It's on the house, to wash the dust from your throat. What news from town?' he asked.

'Pretty much as usual,' Edward advised him. 'But it's a recent event close to here that brings me out from the town, on the orders of the county sheriff.'

'Dirty business,' Bluntstone responded. 'You don't know *where's* safe these days. Is it right that he was a judge?'

'I'm afraid so,' Edward confirmed, 'but what makes it worse was that he had a royal escort. Or at least, armed men from the Tower. All six of them were seemingly butchered without hesitation — someone must have been mighty anxious to despatch the man they were escorting.'

'You need to speak to Tom Blower,' Bluntstone said in a lowered voice. 'He lives up by the stream you passed when you came over the bridge on your way in here. He was up the hill, tending his sheep, and he saw what happened — near enough, anyroad.'

'Thank you, I will,' Edward assured him. 'But what about you? Did you see any strangers around the village over the past few days?'

'There are always strangers in here,' said Bluntstone, 'since travellers are always dropping by to refresh themselves on their journey. But we had a few quality folk staying overnight just before that business up the road there.'

'Tell me about them,' Edward requested as he slipped a half angel onto the counter and whispered that he was not seeking another drink.

Bluntstone smiled, thanked him profusely and pocketed the coin. 'There were four of them in all — right gentry, they were, and spending like they weren't worried about making ends meet. They took my only two chambers and had the best food in the house, then plenty of bread and cheese before they rode off the next morning.'

'So they were seemingly wealthy, and were horsed,' Edward summarised. 'Do you recall what they looked like?'

Bluntstone's face creased with the effort of recall. 'They were all richly dressed, and they all had big hats with broad rims. They spoke as if they'd come directly from the queen, and the one that seemed to be leading them kept saying strange things — like those mummers who sometimes come through here, performing for pennies.'

'A strolling player, you mean?'

'Yes, like them. And one of them, while I was serving their suppers, said something to the others along the lines of, "Tomorrow, each man must play his part to perfection." It was a funny thing to say to a load of fellow travellers who seemed to have no shortage of money. But they didn't have servants with them, so altogether it was a bit strange. I offered to send the boy out to carry in their bags, but the fellow in charge told me, quite rudely, to leave well alone, and they carried those heavy bags upstairs as if they were guarding gold bars.'

Edward's mind was racing with the implications. 'Four of them, you say? And they left here on the morning that the judge was killed a little way up the road?'

'Yes — do you reckon it might have been them who did it?'

'Possibly, but I need to find out more. What was the name of that shepherd living by the bridge, did you say?'

'Blower. Tom Blower. You can't miss his place — it's just by the side of the stream on the other side of the bridge that you came in on, assuming you came directly from the town.'

Fifteen minutes later, Edward was seated alongside Tom Blower on the dusty ground in front of his cottage door. Tom was carving a lump of old leather into a new sole for his shoe as he nodded in response to Edward's question.

'Yes, I saw it. Wish I hadn't, but I did.'

'So what *did* you see?'

'I was at the top of the hill that overlooks where the road goes through Witch's Gap, as they call it. The sheep are all dropping their lambs at this time of year, see, and you need to be there all the time to make sure they don't get into difficulty. I saw these four fellows who looked like country parsons disappearing into the trees on this side of the track, taking their horses with them. Next thing I hear this almighty bang, and a big old oak tree comes flying down and lands across the track as it winds through the gap. I could see there was a coach coming from the direction of Kinoulton, with soldiers riding all round it, and I wondered if there was going to be an accident. But the coach driver must have seen it, because he pulled on the rein. Then another tree fell onto the track behind the coach, and the soldiers started falling off their horses, and these wild-looking sorts came leaping out of the trees and set about what was left of the soldiers, before pulling the fellow out of the coach and cutting him to shreds. Then the men who did it pulled the horses out of the trees and rode off towards the town.'

Edward had been listening intently. 'So there were four men dressed like country gentlemen who dismounted from their horses, which they hid in the trees. Then a tree fell in front of the coach, followed by one falling behind it. Then the soldiers guarding the coach were killed, along with the man inside it, by men who were dressed differently? Is that right?'

'As best I saw it, yes. The men who did the killing looked wild — they were dressed in animal skins. They looked like they'd been hiding in those trees for months.'

'Outlaws, you mean?'

'Yes, them.'

'And how many men did you see carrying out the killings?'

Tom thought carefully, then replied, 'Four.'

'And the four who you saw going *into* the trees before any of this happened — did you see them again?'

'No, come to think of it.'

'So it could have been the *same* four, dressed in disguises?'

'Yes, I suppose so. I never thought of that, although I was damned careful to make sure the wood was empty before I came down and saw what they'd done. Horrible, it was! I've never seen anything like it, and I never want to again, I can tell you.'

'So what did you do next?'

'I went looking for Jack Prentice, the local constable. His missus reckoned I'd find him visiting the local farrier to get his horse seen to, but he wasn't there. I left word for him, but it was after dark when he came to my cottage and asked what I'd seen.'

'And this was after dark on the day when it happened?'

'That's right.'

'Thank you, Tom. That's helped me a great deal to get an idea of what happened.'

'Think nothing of it — it's my duty. I hope you catch them, and that they won't be back. My wife's scared to let me out the door since it happened.'

'I don't think they'll be back in these parts, Tom, if it's any consolation,' Edward advised him as he rose to leave. 'Where will I find Jack Prentice?'

'His cottage is on the other side of the village, next to the church. But they reckon he's most often found around Mill Cottage, just down the stream alongside Henry Baxter's grain mill. That's where I went looking for him when he wasn't at the farrier's that day, but Joan Baxter opened the door and told me she hadn't seen Jack all day.'

'Very well, I might try there as well,' Edward replied coldly, 'since it would seem that your local constable can be hard to locate when he's needed.'

2

'How went your enquiries?' Holles asked eagerly when Edward reported back. The sun was sinking fast, its last rays filtering through the mullioned windows of the chamber in which the board was being laid for supper. Edward had yet to return across the courtyard to his own chambers, and the aromas of freshly baked bread and cooked meats were making his stomach rumble, but he was anxious to give an early account of what he had learned.

'I may begin with the observation that Costock is in urgent need of a new constable,' Edward replied sourly.

Holles's face betrayed his impatience. 'A man called Prentice? It was he who first alerted me to what had happened. He journeyed into town bearing the bodies in two carts belonging to the local miller.'

'I believe he often makes use of something else belonging to the miller,' Edward replied with a smirk.

'Your meaning?'

'When the man who had actually seen what took place went in search of our gallant constable, he was nowhere to be found. Prentice's wife was of the belief that he had taken his horse to the local farrier, but enquiry there revealed that the forge was closed for the day, on account of the farrier having a chill. Then when my witness took himself to the house of the local miller — a man called Henry Baxter — which Prentice was known to frequent, he was assured by the miller's wife that she had not seen the constable all day. By the time word was finally relayed to Prentice, the road had been blocked by the bodies and fallen trees for the remaining hours of daylight, which was why it was no doubt late on the second day before the bodies found their way here.'

'Indeed it was. Word did not reach me until Prentice himself brought me the sad tidings at daybreak today. The bodies may be viewed in the yard to the rear of the Shire Hall, by the way, about which I'll tell you more soon. But do I gather that there was something suspicious regarding the absence of the constable from his duties? Do you suspect him of involvement in the dreadful deed?'

'No,' said Edward. 'I suspect him of nothing more than dereliction of duty. On this rare occasion upon which his services were required, he was dallying with the miller's wife. She eventually admitted to me that while her husband was away delivering his finished grain to their customers, our brave constable was tumbling with her in their cottage. She lied regarding his whereabouts when my witness — a worthy shepherd called Blower — went looking for him. To make his absence more credible, and the reason for it less obvious, Prentice waited until sunset to sneak from the miller's cottage and seek out Blower to learn what had happened. By then night had fallen, the road to Nottingham was blocked, and the only one to benefit from the delay was the local innkeeper.'

'So we are now a day behind in our enquiries — that is all,' Holles reasoned in an effort to lessen the disgust that flavoured Edward's every word. 'So pray enlighten me regarding what your witness — the shepherd — saw.'

'A curious business altogether,' Edward said as he accepted the glass of wine offered to him by the steward and took a seat at the table. 'The local innkeeper speaks of four men, richly attired and well supplied with coin, who lodged with him on the night prior to the attack on the judge's train. They were, it seems, anxious to retain control over the heavy bags that they brought with them, and which I suspect contained weapons and disguises. According to the innkeeper, their conversation indicated that they were wandering players, although they were travelling by horse, which is not normally a luxury enjoyed by such lowly mummers. They were heard to speak of roles that they would be playing on the morrow, although from what I could learn there were no mountebanks performing locally for coins on the day of the outrage.'

'But you believe them to have been responsible for what followed?'

'I account it a distinct possibility, since shortly before the attack four men answering that same description were seen to be concealing their horses in the trees to the side of where it occurred. It is known locally as Witch's Gap, and is ideal for an ambush, being a narrow, wooded defile through which the Nottingham road winds on its way north.'

'So what transpired?' Holles urged him.

'This is where it becomes curious,' Edward continued. 'A shepherd on the hill to the east of the gap saw the attack taking place, but speaks only of four men dressed as wild hermits or outlaws who seem to have been responsible for the felling of the trees that hemmed in both the judge's coach and its escort, followed by the bloody ambush. My witness saw nothing further of the four richly dressed men who had earlier entered the trees prior to concealing their horses. Those responsible for the slaughter then left on horseback, and it does not require a great stretch of the imagination to conclude that the four richly dressed men chose to don disguises that made them resemble rural footpads prior to engaging in their vile acts.'

'But why don disguises, since they left none alive as witnesses to their true identities?'

'They were not to know that their mission would be so successful, and their main target, we must assume, was Justice Mortley. There was also the possibility — as proved to be the case — that others would witness what they were about. Their use of disguises suggests that their identities would be known in the locality.'

Holles shuddered. 'It is terrible to contemplate that those inspired to such wickedness might be found in our county. But that reminds me — the body of the judge is to be conveyed by covered wagon back down to London, so should you wish to view it you should do so before the sun has risen far on the morrow. You should also be advised that Justice Brigham arrived in your absence, and declined the safe sanctuary of Thurland Hall. Instead he is accommodated in the judges' lodgings close by St Mary's Church. The assize will proceed as scheduled on Monday morning, when I will of course be required to take my ceremonial place alongside His Honour on the bench. It will therefore be necessary for you to report the results of your further enquiries at this hour each day. Where will you proceed next?'

'At first light I shall examine the bodies,' Edward replied with a grimace. 'Then I will probably journey back south to Costock to view again the place where the outrage occurred. Since the following day will be Sunday, I might take Elizabeth down to our plot of land in Whitefriars Lane, to view progress on our house foundations and to take dinner with Francis Barton across the road.'

'It is all to the good that you enjoy the ready friendship of your fellow bailiff for the town,' said Holles, 'since those responsible for this latest outrage may well be skulking here. You and he once shared that house of his, did you not?'

'Yes indeed, since your predecessor contributed to its upkeep, being of the same belief as yourself — that if the bailiffs of town and county can work together, then this bodes well for the enforcement of justice. I shall of course alert Francis to what has happened, and request that he keep an ear to the ground regarding strangers in our midst. He maintains a fruitful line of information from local prostitutes to whose activities he turns a blind eye. And so I bid you a good evening, Master, and trust that you enjoy your supper as much as I intend to enjoy mine.'

'I'm afraid they're beginning to smell a bit,' the senior turnkey complained the following morning as he led Edward out into the dusty rear yard of the Shire Hall that was occasionally used to allow exercise to those incarcerated in the cells. It was also used for hangings when the risk of public disorder prevented them from being conducted in their usual location on the front steps. 'Some fellows came for the judge's body first thing, but the rest are still there. We're waiting for word that we can chuck them into the ground across the road at St Mary's.'

Edward took a deep breath as he prepared to make a cursory examination of the still liveried remains of the Tower guards who'd lost their lives in their attempt to defend a judge. His gorge rose as his eyes lit upon the one minus its head, with a circle of dried blood and tissue around the ragged neckline. Then he looked quickly, and gratefully, away as he caught sight of the causes of death of four of the others. One of them had a crossbow bolt buried in his throat, while the others had bolts in their upper torsos. These soldiers had clearly preferred to take the risk of being unprotected rather than ride through a warm afternoon encumbered by a cuirass.

'Do you have any military experience?' Edward asked the turnkey.

'Yes, I was over in Ireland for a few years, in the garrison at a place called Waterford. Then I was pensioned off to this job — why do you ask?'

'Because I stood in the Earl of Leicester's infantry at Tilbury, awaiting a Spanish Armada that never came,' Edward explained. 'Before that, I was a Captain in the Leicestershire Trained Band. But in neither service did I ever see a crossbow being used — did you?'

'Can't say I did, but weren't they the weapons used by outlaws in Sherwood Forest? The ones that fought against King John?'

'That was a few years ago now,' Edward reminded him. 'And although one of these poor wretches clearly had his head dispatched with a sword, the remainder seem to have fallen prey to crossbow bolts. A strange choice of weapon, although they were reckoned to be very useful at close range when used by men who could be quickly trained, and they didn't require either the skill or the strength of a longbowman. Anyway, I've seen enough, thank you.'

Edward walked back inside, deep in thought. Those responsible for the vicious bloodshed at Costock were not only cruel, he concluded, but they obviously had a taste for the theatrical. Either that or they didn't have access to either longbows or those skilled in their use. They had clearly intended to put paid to their quarries from a safe distance, like hunters bringing down deer, but the means they had adopted were both cowardly and amateur.

Three hours later Edward was back in Costock, standing in the centre of the track that wound through Witch's Gap and recreating the dreadful scene in his imagination. The two fallen trees had been heaved to the side of the track with the aid of local plough horses, but it was still all too obvious how, when dropped directly across the track, they had effectively hemmed in the armed escort and the eminent official with whose safety they had been entrusted. Then the hail of crossbow bolts had been fired in a swift and deadly sequence, followed by close butchery with a broadsword. Edward cast aside his rage for long enough to step into the heavily wooded area on the eastern side of the track in search of anything the murderers might have left behind.

There was every possibility that they'd left something, given the swiftness with which they'd changed their appearance. Since they would have wished to escape from the scene of their butchery with all speed, they would probably have stuffed their rich clothing into saddlebags in advance of their foul deeds and ridden away immediately afterward. In such circumstances it was not out of the question that something might have been dropped that could give a hint as to their identities.

Edward's instinct and perseverance were rewarded within the first hour, when he came across a broad-brimmed hat. It was of the type described by innkeeper Richard Bluntstone as having been worn by his guests the night before the murders. It was barely covered by fallen leaves, and given its bright red band it stood out clearly. Edward wondered how he might, on some future date, match the hat to a suspect. Then he lifted it from the ground and made an even more important discovery.

Lying under the hat was a prayer book bound in calf leather, so richly engraved that it must have had a wealthy and pious owner. The contents were clearly in Latin, a language that Edward had seen in written form during his orphanage days but which he had never been taught. But even he could deduce that some sort of dedication page had been pasted inside the front cover, and he gently dusted off the few grains of soil that were partly obscuring the inscription. It read:

Collegio Romano
Quia Ordinis in Honore
Ricardo di Lindum

It was clearly an important link to one of the men who had been here. If, over the course of his investigations, Edward came across a man with this grand Italian name, he would take pleasure in having his hands and feet bound together and ordering that he be carried upside-down and paraded through the streets between two packhorses.

And even that would be charitable, given the brutality shown to Justice Mortley and his escort.

As the lone bell of St Nicholas's Parish Church announced the departure of its Sabbath worshippers, Edward placed an arm around Elizabeth's waist and squeezed gently.

'You can already see the basic dimensions, my love. Now that the finer weather is upon us, the carpenters may begin dropping the timbers into the brick base that you can see marked out. By the time autumn returns, we shall be installed in our own residence.'

They were standing side by side in Whitefriars Lane, next to the plot of land where their future home was being built. Opposite was the house that Edward had formerly shared with Francis Barton, bailiff to the Sheriff of Nottingham. The authorities had deemed it convenient for both bailiffs to be accommodated within the same building, given that their adjoining jurisdictions called for close co-operation. In the same spirit, after Edward had married Elizabeth Sir John Holles had prevailed upon the Lord Lieutenant of the County to provide the finance for a new house for the county bailiff. It had been agreed that a certain sum would be deducted from Edward's monthly stipend by way of repayment, and the calculation was that within five years the house would revert to Edward's ownership, assuming that he was still in office by that date.

'Shall we have the money to furnish it?' Elizabeth asked hesitantly as she came to appreciate how spacious their new accommodation would be.

Edward smiled and kissed her cheek. 'Indeed we shall, and we shall have your choice of furnishings. These things are best left to the mistress of the household.'

Elizabeth swelled with pride just as a commanding voice rang out from behind them.

'If the two lovebirds can be prised apart for long enough, dinner is being served across the road.'

Edward smiled in recognition of the familiar voice and turned to shake Francis's hand. 'I hope that your houseboy cooks as well as Dickon once did.'

The reference to their former young servant brought back sad memories for them both. Dickon had been stabbed to death during his attempt to prevent the deliberate burning of the bailiffs' house. The fire had been intended to kill both bailiffs as they slept and had triggered a joint search for those responsible. The experience and mutual trust that both men had acquired in that process had been invaluable as they joined forces to combat even greater evils, one of which had led to Edward meeting Elizabeth.

'So how goes married life?' Francis enquired an hour later, as he carved a chunk from the roast lamb in the centre of the table, while the domestic servant, John, poured them all small beer. Elizabeth flushed slightly with embarrassment while Edward sought a suitable reply.

'It is certainly preferable to hazarding one's health in the stews in which you seek bodily action,' he said with a grin.

'I set great store by what I learn from those ladies whose favours are by no means exclusive,' said Francis. 'But I do not partake of such favours; rather, I have what you might call "arrangements" with a certain widow not far from this place whose appreciation of my attentions never dims. But looking at the two of you, I am reminded that marriage can be a blessing for some, and I rejoice that you two found each other.'

Neither Edward nor Elizabeth needed any reminder of those uncertain days when they had been meeting covertly behind the bushes in the grounds of Wollaton Hall. Elizabeth had been employed there as a lady's maid to the daughter of the house, Lady Bridget. Edward had initially been drawn there to investigate the poaching of deer from the estate, but in the process he had so far antagonised Sir Francis Willoughby, Elizabeth's employer, that he had been banned from the estate.

Then the abduction of several town prostitutes from a low alehouse at the foot of the castle rock had obliged Edward to seek the intervention of Robert Devereux, the Earl of Essex, while he was a house guest of Sir Francis. When it was established that the abducted women were being taken north by Essex's rival for the queen's favour, Robert Cecil, as a gift for King James VI of Scotland, Edward and Essex had rescued them before the gift could cause embarrassment to Queen Elizabeth. The queen had briefly journeyed north to thank Edward for his actions, and when she had learned of his and

Elizabeth's plight, she had pressured Sir Francis to allow them to marry.

'I hear that a royal justice fell victim to a mob of cut-purses south of the town,' said Francis.

'Yes, there was such an outrage,' Edward confirmed as he cut more meat for Elizabeth and shook it onto her trencher from the end of his knife, 'but I doubt that it was the work of mere vagabonds. There was much about it that smacked of brigandry by a group of gentry who chose to disguise themselves as outlaws. No band of beggars would be so desperate as to take on armed soldiers from the Tower, six of whom were escorting his lordship. I spoke with the landlord of the inn at which they may well have spent the previous night, and he said they were not lacking in funds. Besides, only one of their victims was likely to be possessed of coin.'

'So what do you believe was their motive?' Francis asked. 'Was the death of the justice their true objective?'

Edward shuddered and put down his ale pot. 'Pray to God that it was not that, else the very foundations of law and order in the kingdom are being challenged. This one outrage alone has necessitated that another justice be diverted from Derby in order to take the assize that commences on Monday. You have cases of your own awaiting trial, have you not?'

Francis nodded. 'A robber called Laycock, who slit the throat of a trader on his way out of town with his takings from the Saturday Market, and the wretch Sutton, who violated the daughter of his landlady. But the list is lengthy, I'm advised, so you must have even more of your own.'

'Indeed, it's been a miserable six months since the last assize, and the hangman will be kept busy.'

Elizabeth glared at the two men. 'Is this the way to entertain a lady to dinner, gentlemen? I have no illusions regarding the duties that each of you must perform, but may we not converse about more pleasant subjects? Francis, I was admiring your stone dinnerware — whence did you acquire it, since I would have some of my own when we become neighbours?'

The two men apologised, and the chatter around the table reverted to more domestic themes until the board was cleared by John, and the guests departed with heartfelt thanks for a most delightful repast. Given that Edward had risen at first light in order to survey the bodies of the slain soldiers at the rear of the Shire Hall, they decided on an early light supper, and took to their beds not long after dusk. It was as well that Edward was able to catch up on some sleep, because the sun had not yet risen when he awoke to the sensation of a hand on his shoulder. He turned quickly to seize it in a vice-like grip and its owner yelled in protest, waking Elizabeth.

'A thousand apologies for invading your bedchamber,' said Francis, 'but please let go of my hand before I lose all sensation in it! You must rise and come with me without delay.'

'Did you disturb Meg also?' asked Edward.

Francis nodded. 'She would not enter here in order to disturb your slumber, so the task fell to me.'

'Why, for God's sake?'

'There will be no assize on Monday, Edward — Justice Brigham has been murdered, and we must lose no time in finding the person responsible.'

3

'How and where?' Edward demanded as he struggled to pull on his hose.

'In the judges' lodgings in High Pavement. He was discovered on the floor in his chambers late yesterday evening, and the physician gave instruction to summon me, since it looks as if he was poisoned.'

'But it's a town matter nevertheless,' Edward reminded Francis. 'So why am I being hauled from my slumber?'

Francis's mouth dropped open in disbelief. '*Two* royal justices in the same week? You cannot seriously believe this second death to be a mere coincidence? Someone has clearly given instruction that Nottingham is to have no ongoing machinery for upholding the law. How long before someone is sent from London to investigate how we conduct ourselves?'

'You may be right,' Edward conceded, 'but this might have kept at least until the sun was over the horizon. Why the urgency?'

'The physician is still at the lodgings, and wishes to convey such intelligence to us as he is able. He is also anxious to take to his bed, since he has spent the night guarding the corpse.'

High Pavement was one of the better streets in St Mary's parish, on the south side of the town alongside St Mary's churchyard, and only a few yards down from the Shire Hall where the assizes would have opened with a formal parade and a fanfare in a few hours' time. The assize would now have to be postponed, or perhaps transferred to a neighbouring town.

High Pavement was home to some of the town's more eminent residents, so it was well maintained by the authorities. The gong farmer and his boy were already plying their malodorous trade in the roadway as Edward and Francis dismounted and hitched their horses' bridles to the rail outside the judges' lodgings on the north side of the wide thoroughfare. The door to the lodgings opened before they reached it, and the anxious face of its steward peered out at them.

'Inside, good sirs, and thank you for your attendance. This is a most unfortunate business.'

'You've no idea just *how* unfortunate,' Edward spat back as he stepped into the panelled hallway with Francis two paces behind him. Then he remembered that this was not his jurisdiction and apologised as he turned back to let Francis lead the way.

'This way, sirs,' the steward said as he strode past both men and headed up the main staircase and into a gallery on the first floor that appeared to have several rooms leading off it. He stopped at the door to the second room, knocked politely, then stuck his head round it and announced, 'The bailiff and his man, as you requested.' Then he stood to one side, allowing Francis and Edward to enter the room in that order.

'He's not "my man",' Francis explained to the doleful-looking individual who had seated himself on the window ledge that looked out over the street, 'but the bailiff for the county. His name is Edward Mountsorrel, and he and I have equal authority in this matter, given that it is not the first of its kind this week.'

The man nodded towards the bed. 'I am Doctor Thomas Beveridge, physician of this town and lately of Oxford. The man lying here has been poisoned, as you may see for yourselves if you proceed a little further into the room.'

They did as invited, and the source of the sour smell became apparent as they gazed down at the bulky figure. The corpse was dressed in a nightshirt that was festooned with drying vomit, a considerable quantity of which also lay before him on the boards.

'He also let out a large amount of excrement,' Beveridge added. 'That is a clear indication that something disagreed with him. I believe that "something" to have been Foxglove, given the blueness around the mouth, indicative of a disorder of the heart. When I examined his vomit, I also saw purple flecks of the offending plant in what appears to be the remains of some wine. The man was poisoned less than a day ago, I would guess. They tell me he was a justice.'

'They?' Edward echoed.

The physician nodded towards the still open door. 'The people who run this place, and principally the steward who showed you in here. He seemed extremely nervous about something.'

'You mean *apart* from the fact that someone died while enjoying his hospitality?' Edward asked.

'You two are the representatives of the law, so I'll leave it to you,' said Beveridge. 'I merely pass on what I observed. No additional charge.'

After the physician had taken his leave, Francis went to send word for the judge's body to be removed to the yard of the Guildhall, while Edward escorted the nervous-looking steward into the front chamber on the ground floor. When they were seated and Francis had joined them, Edward fired off the first question that had been forming in his head.

'We are reliably advised that your eminent guest died from poison. Have you any idea how that might have been introduced?'

'What do you mean?' the steward demanded with all the dignity he could muster.

'What he means is, did your guest eat or drink anything during his stay here?' asked Francis. 'Recently, that is — yesterday, since we're aware that he'd resided here for more than one day.'

'Are you suggesting that I poisoned him?'

'Did you?' Edward demanded.

The steward turned pale as he replied defiantly, 'I'm not the cook here. You'd need to speak to Joan Broughton.'

'We most certainly intend to,' Francis confirmed, 'but presumably you are the one who serves whatever drinks your guests may demand?'

'I didn't on this occasion,' the steward began. His eyes dropped to the floor. 'The justice had a visitor yesterday, and it was she who brought in the bottle, although I notice that it is no longer in the chamber where his lordship died.'

During the heavy silence that followed this confession, Edward and Francis exchanged glances and nods.

'You mentioned "she",' Francis replied. 'Would I be correct in assuming that Justice Brigham was entertaining a lady?'

The steward gave a silent nod.

'A lady who might be described as capable of bringing her own entertainment with her?'

A further shamefaced nod from the steward encouraged Francis to keep going.

'In short, a prostitute?'

'It's nothing unusual, or even unlawful,' said the steward. 'These gentlemen are obliged to travel the road for weeks at a time, far from their wives and usual mistresses, and they get lonely. They sometimes have a little female company during their stay under my roof, and this occasion was nothing out of the ordinary.'

'Except that the excitement proved fatal,' Edward remarked.

'Or, more to the point, the wine did,' Francis added.

'I wasn't to know that, was I?' the steward wheedled, now thoroughly alarmed at his predicament.

'So do you normally invite the prostitutes who service your judges to bring along their own refreshment?' Edward enquired sharply, now that he could see the steward crumbling. 'Surely that's something you would normally provide from your own no doubt copious cellar?'

'Ordinarily, yes,' the steward conceded. 'But the woman had the bottle with her when she arrived, and so I merely provided the goblets from which its contents might be consumed. I could hardly have been expected to test it for poison, could I?'

'Indeed not,' Francis agreed, 'but in return for your merciful escape from a horrible death, you will of course be prepared to disclose the name of the lady in question?'

The steward took a deep breath and murmured, 'She said her name was Mary.'

'That will assist us *greatly*,' Francis replied with heavy sarcasm. 'I could produce at least ten women of that name who regularly ply their trade in this town.'

'I didn't think to enquire regarding her other name,' came the grumbling response.

'So you would have us believe that you simply walked out into the street calling for any lady of loose morals who might be prepared to provide an elderly judge with some entertainment of a lustful nature, and who might also be equipped with a bottle of wine? Is that it?' Edward demanded.

'Clearly not,' the steward conceded. 'She was supplied by Mrs Temple, and she arrived without any invitation from me, assuring me that his lordship had requested her attendance.'

Francis snorted derisively. 'Mrs Lavinia Temple, whose selective and expensive brothel is located in Newark Lane? She who would pimp her own daughter if the price were right?'

'I make no observation regarding her personal morality,' the steward muttered.

Edward snorted. 'So you sent word for this "lady" to supply one of her strumpets? Is that what happened?'

'I didn't,' the steward insisted. 'Mary just appeared. What will happen to me?'

'That will be a matter for the sheriff, when I report on what has happened here,' Francis advised him. 'For the moment you might wish to consider seeking an alternative means of earning your livelihood. Out in the road there is a gong farmer who may be looking for a keen assistant. Do not leave these premises until advised by me that you are free to do so; you may employ your time freshening the chamber in which the judge died a messy death. Good day to you.'

Outside in High Pavement Edward nodded towards the Shire Hall, just beyond which was Stoney Street, the thoroughfare they would need to take in order to make their way north to Newark Lane. But it was also the same route that would lead them back past Broad Street and Thurland Hall, and Francis needed little persuasion to accompany Edward back to his chambers for breakfast.

Elizabeth heard them arriving and ordered Meg to lay the board.

'What transpired at the judges' lodgings?' Elizabeth enquired as she joined them at the table. 'Is it true that a second justice has been murdered?'

'So it would seem,' said Edward. 'We believe he was poisoned by a bottle of wine brought into his chamber by one of the town prostitutes who'd been summoned to see to his carnal needs.'

'If he had not gone that way, the pox might well have taken him in due course. There is always a price to be paid for such fornication,' said Elizabeth.

'This was a higher class prostitute, it would seem,' Edward advised her. 'She was hired from one of the best brothels in town, which Francis and I must visit once we have broken our fast.'

'Why you?' Elizabeth demanded suspiciously. 'If a man dies in town, it is surely a town matter, is it not?'

'Ordinarily, yes, but do you recall the butchering of Justice Mortley in Costock late last week? This second death is no coincidence, I suspect. There is clearly some sort of intrigue afoot to rid the nation of those who sit to pass sentence in the gravest matters — matters that ordinarily attract the noose. Francis and I must work together to bring those responsible to book. It is probably only a matter of a week or so before someone will appear among us bearing Her Majesty's authority to make the same enquiry. When they do, we need to be able to show progress.'

'Will you be home in time for dinner?' Elizabeth asked. 'And if so, would Francis do us the honour of being our guest?'

'As to the latter, I would be honoured to accept your invitation,' Francis replied with a smile. 'As to the former, we may well be obliged to see to the safe custody of the prostitute who took the poison to the dead man. We will also need to obtain from her a confession as to who inveigled her into it. It cannot be supposed that she acted out of motives of her own.'

34

'Will you torture her?' Elizabeth asked in a quavering voice, her hand to her mouth.

Edward tutted. 'Do you take us for butchers? I would have hoped that you knew me better.'

'Forgive me, my sweet, but you said the matter is of interest to those who rule the nation. I have heard that in such matters, those who interrogate prisoners do not shrink from inflicting horrible tortures on their bodies.'

'That is at the Tower of London,' Francis told her glumly. 'We are not employed there, and we do not stoop to such methods. But whoever "Mary" may prove to be, she would be well advised to tell us all that she knows, rather than oblige us to hand her over to the Constable of the Tower, should we be ordered so to do.'

'There have been days during our brief marriage when it has occurred to me that I might have been happier wed to a merchant or a parson,' Elizabeth said, glaring at Edward as she rose from the table and dabbed her mouth. 'And today is one of those days,' she added as she swept from the room.

'There really is no need for you to accompany me to Mistress Temple's brothel,' Francis assured Edward, embarrassed by the scene he had witnessed.

Edward shook his head defiantly. 'I thank you for your concern, but you may leave it to me to remind my wife that I was employed in this same office when we first met. Added to which, the death of Justice Brigham comes too close upon the death of Justice Mortley for me to be satisfied that there is no connection between them. The same treasonous urge lies behind both wicked deeds, and to uncover the source of one I must investigate the other. So let us be on our way.'

It was barely mid-morning when Francis kicked open the door to the three-storey mansion that sat almost out in the country, but inside the north-easternmost line of the old town walls that were now in a state of disrepair. A sleepy dog opened one eye to survey them suspiciously before a lady well past the first flush of youth bustled into the entrance hall in which they were standing. Her broad smile evaporated when she recognised Francis.

'Tired of Widow Timberlake, are we?' she sneered. 'You'll find that my young ladies cost more than your average town goose, and we don't do two at a time. One man, one woman, assuming that I can raise a couple from their well-earned rest.'

'You would do well to sweeten your tongue,' Francis replied haughtily, 'since I am in two minds over whether or not to simply throw you into the Guildhall cells without enquiry. While I decide, pray welcome my colleague Edward Mountsorrel, bailiff to the Sheriff of Nottinghamshire. We are both here to enquire regarding a lady whose body you hire out. She calls herself "Mary", whether that be her name or not.'

'Do you speak of Mary Chalmers?' asked Mistress Temple.

'I speak of whichever Mary you despatched to the judges' lodgings in High Pavement sometime after the dinner hour yesterday.'

'That was Mary Chalmers — one of the, shall we say, more "obliging" of our company. What of her?'

'Whence came the wine?' Francis enquired.

'What wine?' Mistress Temple frowned. 'Do you mistake this for a vintners' hall? We supply female flesh only, as you are well aware, so why do you ask about wine?'

'When Mary Chalmers arrived at the lodgings, she was carrying a bottle of wine, according to the steward of that establishment,' said Edward. 'You say that it was not supplied by you?'

'I do say that, and I enquire again as to what relevance it may have to the fact that Mary was sent to bring pleasure to an old man?'

'The wine was poisoned,' Edward replied angrily, 'and the justice is dead.'

If Mistress Temple was shocked, or even concerned, it didn't show. Her only response was, 'Are you sure that undue exertion was not the cause of his demise? Mary has been known to buck like a horse being broken to the saddle if so inspired.'

'Enough of this prevarication!' Francis yelled. 'You are being taken in charge for running a bawdy house.'

'I was running a bawdy house when you were still at your mother's breast,' Mistress Temple protested, 'and I am not normally taken in charge for it, even though the nature of what goes on in here is well known to those who govern this town. It should be, since most of them make use of it.'

'Where will we find Mary Chalmers?' Edward demanded.

Mistress Temple jerked her head in the direction of the staircase that led to the upper floors. 'Up there on the first floor. The first chamber on the left, the one that overlooks the garden.'

'Remain where you are,' Francis instructed her as he walked swiftly after Edward, who reached the chamber door ahead of him. Edward knocked, and Francis laughed.

'She's not one of the queen's ladies. Just push it open.'

Edward did as suggested, then stopped dead. Francis almost collided with him in the doorway, then followed Edward's eyes to the ceiling as his jaw dropped.

Running down the centre of the plaster and lathe ceiling was a heavy oak beam, and dangling from it was the body of a woman who had perhaps been in her late twenties before she'd seemingly tied a noose around her neck, secured the other end of the rope to the beam, and launched herself into eternity. She was dressed in street clothing, as she must have been when she'd presented herself to the justice the previous afternoon. She was now purple in the face, with her tongue lolling out of one side of her mouth.

'Two corpses in as many hours,' Francis muttered to Edward. 'I don't know about you, but I've had better days.'

4

'Why would she do that?' Edward asked as they gazed forlornly at the body.

Francis's eyes narrowed as he replied, 'What makes you think that she did?' He nodded at the contents of the room. 'Unless she was possessed of the skills of a fairground tumbler, ask yourself how she got up there. The bed is alongside one wall, and the only other piece of furniture is that sad little cupboard in the far corner, which no doubt contains her only worldly possessions. How did she contrive to get herself up there in the first place? And even if she did, how did she leap to her death when there was nothing to leap *from*? She was clearly hoisted up there, probably after she had already died by some other means. We must send for a physician before we even attempt to cut her down.'

'And we clearly have other questions we must put to Mistress Temple,' Edward snarled as he turned on his heel and ran down the staircase.

Mistress Temple was standing at the bottom with a sour expression on her face. 'Did she not confirm what I told you? And may I now go about my business?' she demanded.

Edward lost his temper. 'She's dead! She was robbed of her life so that you might pocket a few pennies a time while she exposed her frail body to all manner of disease and indignity! I ought to run you through!'

'Steady yourself, Edward,' Francis warned him as he reached the bottom of the stairs.

'Dead, you said?' Mistress Temple asked in a shaking voice. 'At whose hand?'

'That is for us to determine,' said Francis. 'Not by her own hand, certainly. So if you wish to avoid being taken up for her murder, then we require certain information from you without delay. We also need the services of a physician — who do you normally summon when one of your women is in need of physic, if only to rid her of the pox?'

'James Morton,' she replied hoarsely. 'He bides in Swine Green, close by the town wall.'

'Have him summoned,' Francis ordered her, 'then let us adjourn to your pantry, and you can talk yourself out of a well-deserved hanging.'

'Georgie!' Mistress Temple called loudly. A ragged, barefoot boy appeared and was despatched to bring the physician to the house. Mistress Temple was then led into a malodorous chamber to the rear of the house that she assured them was her parlour. She was ordered to sit on one of the stools to the side of a rickety table, which was still laid with the ripe-smelling leftovers of a meal. There was also a stone jug, which Francis lifted to sniff its contents. He then put it down hastily with an expression of disgust.

'You were correct in one particular,' he said, glaring at their prisoner. 'This is no vintners' hall. What *is* that smell?'

'Corn brandy. Would you care to sample some?'

'Do we give the impression that we wish to expire on duty?' Francis demanded. 'That piss would fell an ox, but no doubt you supply it to your women so that they might drink themselves into a stupor before servicing your customers.'

'Is that what Mary took with her to the judges' lodgings?' Edward asked.

Mistress Temple shrugged. 'I know not what she took with her. Certainly nothing from here, and I recall that the man who called for her had something concealed within his cloak.'

'This man,' Edward persisted. 'Who was he, and what was his request?'

'I'd never seen him before, but he spoke like a town man. He said that he had been sent by the steward of the judges' lodgings, and that it was Mary who was required, in order that a judge might enjoy her services.'

'He asked for her by name?' Francis enquired with raised eyebrows. 'He did not simply demand one of your best prostitutes?'

'No, it was Mary in particular. I was happy to oblige him, since Mary is one of my best women, and I can demand a full half angel for her services.'

'You *could*, you mean!' Edward snarled. 'You must no doubt be mightily inconvenienced by losing such a fine investment. How much of that money would Mary be allowed?'

'My terms of engagement are none of your business,' Mistress Temple insisted.

'Did Mary have any further assignations once she returned here?' Francis asked.

'There was one man, and again he asked for Mary by name, so I simply sent him up to her room once I had taken his money. He left less than an hour later, looking suitably satisfied.'

'Was this the same man who had called for her earlier?'

Mistress Temple shrugged. 'I don't think so, but then I didn't engage him in lengthy conversation.'

'No, you were too intent on taking his money!' Edward yelled, red in the face.

The tension was broken by the ragged Georgie poking his head round the door to announce that the physician had arrived. Francis and Edward turned to leave the room.

Once they were back in Mary's former room, the physician stared morosely up at the swinging corpse. 'Mary Chalmers,' he murmured, almost in reverence. 'Such a sad end, but one that she no doubt willingly embraced.'

'You knew her?' Francis asked.

'I know them all, since I am physician to the house.'

'You're a pox doctor?' Edward enquired sourly, still overcome with rage and pity.

James Morton shot him an angry look. 'Before you mount your moral high horse, allow me to introduce you to some of the bitter realities of life here in this cesspit of a town. Do you think the women who ply their trade here do so out of choice? Take Mary — a beautiful young woman who I helped to bring into this world when her mother experienced some difficulty with her birth. The first of many such births, all of which I attended. Mary was the first, and it must be almost twenty years or so since that night.'

'Mary was barely twenty?' Edward asked in disbelief. 'I would have put her age at nearer thirty.'

'She fell victim to the ravages of her trade, and of the liquor to which she was sadly addicted. But who can blame her, given that she was cast out from her home when she was barely fifteen?'

'Were there too many children for the family to feed?' Edward asked.

'No — her father was a wealthy leather merchant. They had a fine house in Carter Gate, and were pious church attenders, if somewhat inclined towards the old religion. No, the reason for Mary's rejection by her family was that she conceived a child when she was barely out of childhood herself. I also helped to deliver that baby — a daughter, as I recall. You will now find the infant in the local poorhouse, where Mary was obliged to leave her when she was living hand to mouth in alleyways and gutters. Then she was found by Mistress Temple and put to her evil designs.'

'Mary would not be the first woman in this town to be deceived by a man, then abandoned,' Francis pointed out. 'Where was the Christian charity of her own mother?'

Morton sighed and blushed slightly. 'That charity was withdrawn when she learned that Mary's child's father was also its grandfather.'

It fell silent until Edward gave a howl of rage and punched a hole in the wattle wall.

Morton nodded in sympathy. 'I cannot help but share your just outrage, my friend. Should you have broken anything just then, I am an excellent setter of bones.'

Francis diverted the conversation to a more immediate topic. 'We did not summon you here for sad histories, Master Morton. Nor are we inclined to believe that this poor wretch took her own life. Please would you examine her corpse for indications of how she might have been rendered helpless before being strung up to make her death look self-inflicted?'

Morton nodded. 'I shall require your assistance in lowering her body.'

It was the work of a brief moment to bring her down. Edward and the physician took the weight of her body, such as it was, while Francis cut through the rope with a knife that normally hung from his belt. Between them, they laid her almost reverently on the dusty floor.

'I've known dogs that weighed more,' Edward remarked, on the verge of tears.

'She barely ate these past few months, such was her addiction to that swill that Mistress Temple brews in her scullery,' said Morton. 'All the women consume it, both to counter the pangs of hunger and to dim their senses regarding what they are obliged to do.' He examined the body and indicated a large lump on the back of Mary's head, clearly visible through her lank, light auburn hair. 'See here? There's a lump the size of a cabbage, which would have been sufficient to render her unconscious, if not to kill her outright, such was the frailty of her skull. Clearly it was meant to look as if she'd taken her own life, but I can advise you that your suspicion was correct. She was murdered.'

Without thinking Edward made the sign of the cross, then looked up with an anxious expression at the other two men. 'Please overlook my weakness just then, gentlemen. I am no secret Papist, but I was raised by Catholic brothers in an orphanage, and it was the way we were taught. In times of stress I revert to it without thinking.'

'Whatever brings you comfort,' Morton replied. 'For myself it is brandy, and if you have no further need of my services, then I shall resort to a glass at home.'

Edward and Francis thanked him profusely, and instructed him to send his bill to Mistress Temple. Then they sent the boy Georgie down to the Guildhall for two constables and a cart to transport Mary's body to the yard in which unclaimed bodies were stored.

Edward wiped a silent tear from his cheek. 'I assume that there would be little point in advising Mary's family of her fate?'

'None whatsoever,' Francis agreed, 'but I suggest that you would benefit greatly from being reacquainted with your own hearth. I have never seen such a pitying side to your nature.'

'That's because you were never an orphan,' Edward replied. 'But you are correct; what I most crave now is some dinner, which you are invited to share, and the loving comfort of my wife.'

They strolled into the main chamber of Edward and Elizabeth's quarters just as Meg was laying out the trenchers ahead of serving dinner. Elizabeth was watching from her chair by the empty fireplace, and she rose and leaned towards Edward in expectation of the usual warm kiss. She looked both surprised and hurt when he merely dabbed at her cheek with cold, dry lips and walked up the staircase with a heavy tread.

'We just had to deal with another body — this time that of the young woman who almost certainly poisoned Justice Brigham with the corrupted wine,' explained Francis. 'Whether she did so deliberately or not, we shall perhaps never know. But something about this second death seemed to distress Edward deeply, and he hardly spoke as we travelled back here. I suspect that he is in urgent need of comfort — perhaps you can persuade him to eat, and then unburden himself. We are unlikely to be able to further our enquiries until his black mood has lifted. I have never seen him thus affected.'

Instructing Meg to serve Francis with some beer, and then continue serving the meal, Elizabeth slipped upstairs. Edward was seated on their bed, staring out of the mullioned window. She sat beside him and put her arm around his shoulders. 'What is it, my love?' she asked gently.

A tear slid down Edward's cheek as he replied without looking at her. 'The young woman who died was not yet twenty years old, and she had already been betrayed by her own father, disowned by her mother, and forced to give up her child. She was obliged to sell herself to men in order to stay alive. Now she has been beaten on the head and made to look like one who had committed the grave sin of suicide.'

'You have seen dead bodies before,' Elizabeth reminded him gently. 'Why should this one cause you to brood so?'

He didn't reply directly, but spoke to the window glass as if he was alone. 'Perhaps it would have been better if I *had* been a merchant or a country parson. Not someone who deals in death and deceit, and whose wife is saddened by his need to be away from her side, probing the middens created by the wicked misdeeds of others.'

'Forgive me, my sweet.' She leaned across and kissed his cheek. 'I was speaking from my own selfish desire to have you home and around me the entire day. All men must work to provide for their loved ones, and yours is the most honourable of professions. I have never known anyone so strong, so noble, so pure of spirit, or so dedicated to the public good.'

Edward smiled weakly and turned to look at her. 'The woman had been rejected by her mother — the one who, above all, should have shown her love and held her close. She was, in her own way, an orphan just like myself. Learning of her situation brought back all those dark days when I would ask myself why I was so unworthy, so unloved, that my own mother had abandoned me in the street.'

'From what you once disclosed to me,' Elizabeth said, 'she left you in a church doorway, where you were sure to be found. And what do you know of the circumstances that brought that about? What dark misfortune led to her needing to part with

46

the only bright light in her life? A mother would only give up her infant for the best of reasons, and for the ultimate benefit of that infant.'

'Perhaps you are correct,' Edward conceded.

Elizabeth slipped from the bed, knelt before him, took both his hands in hers and laid her head in his lap with a smile. 'I *know* I am correct. I am also hungry, and you are a poor host, leaving our guest to dine alone. Please take my hand and join us for dinner, before we both starve to death.'

As the uneasy silence threatened to dominate the entire meal, Edward put down the knife that he had just loaded with fish and smiled across at Francis.

'My sincere apologies for my black humour earlier. I have given my reasons, and hopefully the dark shadows of memory have now flown off. We must now determine how we are to proceed, if Elizabeth will forgive me.'

'There is nothing to forgive, if it means that you will be bringing wickedness to heel,' she assured him. 'So what do you propose to do next?'

'I have been giving the matter some thought,' Francis replied as he speared a pork slice on his knife. 'I am prepared to believe the steward at the lodgings when he assures us that he did not summon Mary Chalmers, and — with some regret — I am prepared to forego the opportunity of consigning Mistress Temple to a gaol cell. I can accept her explanation that the man who summoned Mary to her assignment with Justice Brigham was sent by the steward of the lodgings, though I think she was lied to. The man was probably already armed with the poisoned wine, and I believe he instructed Mary to offer it to their victim but to partake of none of it herself.'

'Could it not be the case that whoever took her to meet with the judge intended that she should also partake of the wine?'

Edward enquired. 'If she had, then there would have been no need to return to her room and hang her like a common criminal. But perhaps the judge succumbed too quickly to the poison, and Mary fled from the lodgings in panic — so it proved necessary to send someone round there to silence her.'

'The murderer may have been the same man who took her to the judge,' said Francis. 'The brothel keeper was unable to say with certainty that it was not.'

'Why do you think two justices have been done to death in a single week?'

'Their killers clearly intended to send a message to London that they have no respect for the fabric of our nation and its institutions,' Edward replied.

Francis looked doubtful. 'Perhaps they simply wished to prevent our assize taking place,' he suggested.

'To what avail?' Edward countered. 'They'll simply send another justice in due course.'

'Like they sent Justice Brigham?' Francis said with a hollow laugh. 'They've killed two justices already, and it would be difficult to persuade any other justice to travel up here, after what happened to them. We are likely to be held severely to account for what has happened here.'

'If Her Majesty, or whoever, will simply send another justice,' said Elizabeth, 'then all that they achieved was a delay to our local assize. Perhaps this was their sole objective?'

Francis and Edward exchanged meaningful stares, and Edward reached out to pull Elizabeth to him. 'You may have found the answer!' he said enthusiastically.

'Is it possible that among those awaiting trial there is some villain influential enough to organise, from a gaol cell, the murder of the two men who might have sentenced him?'

Francis mused. 'Do you have a list of those awaiting trial, Edward?'

'It's in my desk in the Shire Hall,' Edward confirmed. 'And you?'

'Mine is in the Guildhall.'

'Then I believe that we have identified what we must do after we have finished this excellent dinner,' Edward said with a smile. 'And we must thank Elizabeth for both the dinner and the new line of enquiry.'

5

Once Edward and Francis had collected their scrolls, they met at Francis's house in Whitefriars Lane and settled in the back room.

'If ever a bunch of ne'er-do-wells deserved to hang, it's this lot!' Edward announced as he opened the scroll that contained his list for the assizes that had been delayed.

Francis grimaced. 'They'll need to form an orderly queue behind my two. Nottingham will be well rid of them.'

'You have only two?'

'Yes — Robert Laycock first. Here's a perfect choice of a man to choke on the end of a rope on Gallows Hill. Never did an honest day's work in his life, but preferred instead to let others do the work, then rob them of their earnings. Late one Saturday evening just before last Christmas, when the Saturday market takings were likely to be swollen by the season, he hid in an alleyway off Timber Hill and slit the throat of one of the traders who was late in leaving.'

'And the other one?'

Francis shuddered. 'At the risk of provoking one of your black moods, Josiah Sutton is a man you would no doubt wish to hang yourself. He was lodging with a widow in Goose Gate and her daughter. One day, while the widow was out of the house acquiring victuals, he pulled the daughter into his room and violated her. Her screams brought a neighbour running, and Sutton was lucky not to get ripped limb from limb before the constables got to him.'

'Let's examine my five, shall we?' Edward suggested as his blood ran cold. 'Nothing so bad as Sutton, although there's one violator on the list. His victim was a farmer's wife in Arnold who was leading her cow from one pasture to another when he leaped out at her from a hedge. How he expected to escape justice is a mystery, since he was a near neighbour that she knew by sight and name.'

'And the remainder?'

'All robbers of some description, it would seem. Perhaps Richard Crump is our man, since he and an accomplice who has so far escaped justice lay in wait to rob a coach on its way to Newark. Crump was only caught because he was unwise enough to spend too freely in his local alehouse, attracting the suspicion of the village constable. Crump is destined to hang alone, unless he is wise enough to bargain for his life by peaching on his companion.'

'From what you say regarding the man's stupidity, I hardly think that he is likely to have been able to organise the murder of two justices and a town prostitute — unless of course the deeds were done in exchange for his not revealing the identity of his accomplice,' said Francis.

'Well, he's a better prospect than the remaining three, who are all burglars,' Edward replied as he cast his eyes down the list. 'They're only on the assize list because of their "incorrigible" status — like Robert Cropper, who's spent more of his life manacled to a gaol wall than he has living freely in the community. He is as stupid as Crump, it would seem. Having robbed a fine country mansion just outside Cotgrave, he was unwise enough to attempt to sell some very fine silverware at the Saturday market, though it is regularly patrolled by your constables in search of such stolen property.'

'Would that they were all so obliging,' Francis said, chuckling. 'So what of the remaining two? Any likely prospects there?'

'Hardly,' Edward said with a frown. 'Amos Godley broke into his neighbour's barn and stole his milk cow for the third time, despite still bearing the scars from the flogging he received on the previous occasion that he faced the court. He was fairly warned that any repetition would guarantee him the gallows. And finally Job Ridley from Lowdham, who was found insensibly drunk in the taproom of The Partridge after sneaking in the previous night and breaching a barrel of the finest ale — which, given the quality of that alehouse, probably just means that the ale was drinkable. He was lucky to survive the experience, but he will hang because he's been doing it for the past two years, ever since his wife died.'

'So we are no further in our search for someone with the money or influence to orchestrate the murders. It's a sorry mess, and I have to explain myself to my employer sometime today.'

'Do you wish me to accompany you?' Edward offered.

Francis smiled. 'You must have read my mind. It would probably sit better for me if I were able to explain to Master Jowett that this recent series of outrages may have been organised within county boundaries rather than in the town.'

'How reasonable is our new town sheriff?' Edward asked.

'Come with me and find out for yourself. Perhaps it would be best to wrap your head in an armet before doing so.'

Both bailiffs made their way by horse to a finely appointed townhouse in Barker Lane — the home of Edmund Jowett, the Sheriff of Nottingham. They were soon sitting at his drawing room table, with the sheriff seated opposite.

'Your employer speaks highly of you,' Jowett advised Edward, 'but I am at a loss to understand why you are here with my bailiff, unless he feels that he requires a wet nurse on this occasion.'

'He's here to explain how recent deaths in the town are linked to a death south of it,' Francis explained.

Jowett raised a hand to prevent him saying more. 'I feel sure that Master Mountsorrel can speak for himself,' he said gruffly. 'So perhaps he would care to do so.'

Edward cleared his throat and began. 'Last week, as you may be aware, Justice Mortley was murdered on the road into town just north of Costock. His coach was waylaid by a band of four assassins who seem to have been well prepared, and sufficiently well armed to overcome and slaughter six armed escorts from the Tower. Justice Brigham was sent as a replacement, and we have learned that his death was not accidental either. He was poisoned by wine brought in by a local prostitute, and we cannot ask her who put her up to it, because she was done to death only hours afterwards. We are seemingly in the midst of some larger scheme of which we have little knowledge at present, but we are actively investigating.'

'And the ultimate purpose behind all this?' Jowett enquired gloomily.

Edward shook his head. 'We can think of only two at present. The first is that the perpetrators sought to delay the assize that should have begun this morning, which presumably would have required your attendance in your official capacity. But why anyone would wish to delay the inevitable we have yet to fathom, since presumably another justice will be sent north.'

'The only person who is planning to journey north is the queen's secretary, Baron Burghley,' Jowett said with a grimace. 'He has demanded an audience with both myself and Sir John Holles, and we may rest assured that it is not with a view to congratulating us on how we conduct our business. What, pray, is your second theory?'

'It could be some broader attack on the fabric of law enforcement within the nation, of which Nottinghamshire is only the first target,' Edward suggested. 'If that is the case, then it is perhaps as well that London has expressed an interest, since I suggest that we will all be out of our depth in taking on something so treasonous and well organised.'

'You have obviously not had occasion to come under the baleful glare of William Cecil, even in his declining years,' Jowett replied testily. 'Have you anything more hopeful to suggest?'

'No, Master,' said Francis. 'I agree with Master Mountsorrel that all these matters are linked in some way, and that it would be best for us to work alongside each other in the investigation.'

'You will also be required to present yourselves together when the delegation arrives from London,' said Jowett, frowning. 'I assume that Cecil will be accommodated in Thurland Hall, so that will at least mean a short journey for you, Mountsorrel. In the meantime, you would both be well advised to ensure that you are in possession of more agreeable tidings by the day of that meeting. You are both dismissed.'

'Why do I feel like a naughty schoolboy who has just been whipped?' Edward asked as they stood outside Jowett's house, watching the comings and goings along Barker Lane.

'He's always like that,' Francis grumbled. 'I always leave my meetings with him feeling like I have not quite justified my stipend. It's his liver, apparently. The question is, what are we to do next?'

'Did you think that the steward of the judges' lodgings was telling all that he knew?' Edward asked.

Francis shrugged. 'He was certainly mightily guarded about something, but that might simply have been due to the fear of losing his office.'

'Let's go back and rattle his cage,' Edward suggested as he gazed up at the setting sun. 'We have an hour or two left before the streets become even less safe than they are at present, even for us.'

'Are you here to take me into custody?' the steward asked resignedly as he stepped back from the front door to admit the two bailiffs into the judges' lodgings. On enquiry, they had discovered that his name was Matthew Glenning.

'Not yet, and perhaps not at all,' Francis advised him with a smile. 'It may well depend upon the quality of your memory. Is there somewhere we can take the weight from our feet while we seek further information from you?'

They were ushered into a drawing room and invited to sit around the long mahogany table in its centre.

'You say that you did not summon Mary Chalmers here?' asked Francis.

Glenning shook his head. 'No, indeed not.'

'But if his lordship had requested any such service, the house of Mistress Temple would have been your first choice?' Edward added.

Glenning looked wary. 'Yes,' he muttered, 'but I am not in the habit of procuring such services.'

'So did you recognise the young woman who presented herself at your door?' Francis asked.

'No,' said Glenning emphatically.

'And the man with her?' Edward pressed, noting the look of surprise on the steward's face.

'I saw no-one with her, masters,' Glenning replied.

'What was she carrying?' Francis probed.

'A bottle of wine, I believe. I asked if she would require goblets, and when she confirmed that she would, I had them sent up.'

'What were her precise words when she first presented herself at your door?' Edward demanded.

Glenning thought carefully before replying, 'She said that her name was Mary, and that she had been sent by Mistress Temple with what she called "some diversion for your guest".'

'Did she name the guest?'

'No, but since I had only one in residence, I assumed that she meant Justice Brigham.'

'Did it not occur to you that it was strange that she had not been summoned by anyone in your household, and yet there she was, on your doorstep?' Francis asked.

'Not really. I assumed that his lordship had sent the request himself.'

'By what means?' Francis demanded.

Glenning seemed to melt like snow under heat. 'Now that I think the matter through more carefully, it does seem strange, but I must confess that at the time I gave it no thought.'

'So you let Mary in and told her where she would find her customer?' asked Edward.

Glenning shook his head. 'No, I escorted her to the chamber, knocked on the door, and advised his lordship that the young lady was called Mary, and that she had been sent by Mistress Temple as requested.'

'Did his lordship seem surprised?'

'No, to be honest he looked delighted, and he invited Mary into his chamber. The door was closed behind them, and I went about my business.'

'Did you see Mary leave?'

'No, but I believe I heard her. About an hour after I had accompanied her to the judge's chamber I heard light, fast footsteps on the main staircase as I was laying out the trencher ahead of supper. Then I heard the front door opening and closing. I assumed that it was her, but I did not see her.'

'And at what hour of the day would this be?' Francis asked.

'Shortly after five in the afternoon. I remember that, since I had heard St Mary's chiming the hour, and this was the prompt to me to begin laying out the essentials for an early supper, which his lordship had requested. Then when he had not come down two hours later, I went to his chamber and knocked on the door.'

'And then you discovered his body?' Edward prompted.

Glenning shook his head. 'That was later — perhaps nine o'clock. I told the cook that I had reminded his lordship that supper was already on the table, and then I went into my own chamber to eat the supper that she had left for me. It was not until much later, when I walked into this room and realised that nothing had been eaten, that I grew alarmed. The cook goes home after serving supper, you see. Anyway, I went up to the judge's chamber and knocked. When there was no reply, I opened the door a fraction and realised that something smelled bad. I walked into the room, followed the smell, and … and … forgive me, sirs, for it turns my stomach even now to think of what I found on the far side of the bed.' His head sank onto his chest.

'Thank you for your candour,' Francis said calmly. 'You may rest assured that nothing untoward will be reported regarding your dealings in this matter.'

As they stood outside in the street, Edward clucked with frustration. 'We are no nearer an answer, though we have seemingly confirmed that Mary was sent to poison the judge.'

'We cannot be certain that she knew what was in the bottle,' Francis corrected him.

'I did not say that she was acting with intention. If she had been, there would have been no need to murder her later. I think that you were correct in your assumption that whoever sent her believed she would also partake of the wine.'

'Most probably,' Francis agreed. 'Anyway, it has been a long and miserable day, so I will take my leave of you and head home by way of Wheelwright Lane, leaving you to take your mount up Stoney Street. I suggest that we both take the opportunity to get some sleep.'

Robert Cropper looked up with sullen disinterest as the cell door creaked open and the turnkey appeared, holding a flaming torch at head height.

'With me, now — it's all been fixed,' the turnkey whispered hoarsely, 'but keep quiet.'

'What do you want *now*?' Cropper demanded grumpily. 'I'm telling you nothing more than I've told you already, and they'll probably hang me anyway, so go away!'

'You're getting out of here, you daft lummox,' the turnkey replied. 'I don't know how you fixed it, or who your friends are, but shut your trap and follow me.'

Having nothing better to do, Cropper followed the man with the torch along the corridor under the Shire Hall, up two flights of stairs, and down another corridor until they came to a halt in front of a heavy oak door. The turnkey lowered his voice and leaned in to whisper his next instruction.

'This is the tricky bit. We're going out into the yard at the back, and at the far end there's a wall. I've fixed a rope to the top of it, and you can climb down it to the bottom, where a fellow will be waiting to take you to a horse. Then you ride clean away, got it?'

'Who's fixed all this?' Cropper asked, scarcely able to believe his good fortune.

His escort shook his head. 'I don't know, but move, before we get noticed.'

He unlocked the heavy door, and the two men slipped furtively down the yard. There was indeed a rope securely fixed into a bracket on the top of the wall, and the turnkey formed a stirrup with his hands to allow the escapee to reach the top of the wall, then ease himself into a position from which he could slowly inch down the rope. He was dangling over a sixty-foot drop, but a lifetime of breaking into country houses had honed his agility, and within minutes he'd reached the ground. A hoarse whisper announced the presence of a well-dressed man who'd made full use of the shadows.

'Where are we?' Cropper demanded.

'Narrow Marsh,' said the man. 'Come with me, and I'll lead you to your horse.'

Half wondering why his guide spoke with such an educated accent, Cropper followed the man through some of the worst dwellings he'd ever encountered. After a few minutes of ducking and weaving down foetid alleys, they emerged into an open space filled with long, wet grass.

'The East Croft,' said the man. 'We'll follow this northern bank of the Leen River. Your horse is tied to a post under Hethbeth Bridge; from there you can leave town and ride south.'

After what seemed like an hour of stumbling through uneven clumps of vegetation, the arches of Hethbeth Bridge became faintly visible in the reflected glow from the river.

'This is as far as I go,' the man advised Cropper. 'Your horse is under the third arch. Godspeed!'

Thanking him for his services, Cropper hastened forward, his eyes scanning ahead for the outline of a horse. As he stepped under the archway, two men emerged from the gloom ahead of him, and he caught the glint of sword blades.

6

'It's nice to be able to rise from my bed and find that you're still here for once,' Elizabeth advised Edward as she kissed the top of his head and took the seat next to his at the breakfast table.

Edward smiled. 'Make the best of it, my sweet. I do not have the sort of calling in which I can always be sure of when I'll be home.'

'But there must be times when you can delegate your duties to others?' said Elizabeth. 'I miss the open country. Even while living at Wollaton Hall I was able to see beyond my own window, and had something more pleasant to look at than a stable door. When, for example, do you intend to take me to visit my parents, who have never set eyes upon you?'

Elizabeth had been raised on a country estate in Ashby de la Zouch, Leicestershire, where her father had been the steward and her mother the housekeeper. From her mother, Elizabeth had learned how to behave in high class company, a skill that had earned her the post of lady's maid to the daughter of Sir Francis Willoughby at Wollaton.

Given the speed of their courtship and marriage, Elizabeth had not been able to advise her aged parents of her change of status until after the nuptials had taken place. As a mature lady in her mid-twenties, she had not required their consent, but she was eager to prove to them that she had chosen wisely, and grew more frustrated as the weeks following the wedding turned into months. Edward always seemed to have some duty or other that prevented them from riding south for even half a day.

Elizabeth secretly wondered whether Edward's reluctance had something to do with his own early days in Leicestershire, first as an abandoned orphan in a charity hospital maintained by the Church, and then as a humble estate worker on the Grey estate at Groby. There he had shaken off the mud of agriculture to become a career soldier serving under the late Earl of Leicester, who had recommended him for his current position. Only yesterday Elizabeth had been reminded of the bitterness and sense of rejection that still lurked deep within Edward's soul when he recalled his origins.

She was still ruminating on these thoughts when there came a heavy and commanding knock on their front door. She sighed as Meg scuttled away from the breakfast table to answer it. A muffled enquiry from an urgent male voice was followed by Meg's more audible response.

'You'd better step inside, then,' she said.

Edward turned from his place at the table, and there stood one of the town constables.

'Begging your pardon and all, sir, but we've lost a prisoner. I thought it best to let you know without delay.'

'You mean that he escaped while under escort to or from the Shire Hall?' Edward demanded.

'No, sir. It seems that he slipped from his cell during the night.'

'Very well,' Edward sighed. 'As you can see, I'm still at my breakfast, but tell the senior turnkey to expect me within the hour. And tell him that he'd better give a good account of how he guards dangerous criminals.'

'Yes, sir — and thank you, sir,' the man mumbled as he backed away.

Elizabeth smiled reassuringly at Edward. 'Duty calls, does it not?'

'Indeed it does, but not until I've eaten my fill of this excellent breakfast,' said Edward, grateful for her understanding. 'But when those duties permit, we shall indeed take that ride down to Ashby to see your parents. Now, is there any more of this manchet loaf, Meg?'

An hour later, the two turnkeys — one senior to the other — were standing uncomfortably in front of Edward's desk in his chamber at the Shire Hall, a small island of county territory inside the town.

'Well?' Edward demanded. 'Who is missing, when did he go missing, and how in God's name did he get out?'

'It's Robert Cropper, sir, and he seems to have walked out during the night,' the senior turnkey, Will Possett, explained, embarrassment written all over his face.

'Walked out?' Edward thundered. 'I suppose someone had a horse waiting for him at the door, as well? And gave him a few coppers to see him on his way?'

'Don't know how it happened,' Possett admitted. 'I wasn't here, see? And Joe Bilthorpe was home sick, after eating a bad oyster someone gave him, which just left Tom Tapper, and he's gone missing. It wasn't until we came on duty this morning and did the usual checks of the cells that we found out that Tom wasn't here like he should have been, and that there was an empty cell with the door wide open. I sent the boy out to get Tom this morning, and there was nobody at his house, not even his missus.'

'So it comes to this, does it?' Edward summarised with a black scowl. 'The night duty was down to one — Tom Tapper — and somehow, during the night, Tapper went missing along with one of his prisoners, Robert Cropper. Have I missed anything out?'

'No, sir.'

'Does Joe Bilthorpe normally dine on oysters?'

'No idea, sir, but he must be wealthier than I thought if he does.'

'Well, let's assume that he doesn't, and just follow my reasoning here. I believe that someone deliberately gave him a bad oyster, so that he didn't turn up for his night duty. That left Tom Tapper to do whatever he liked, such as unlock a cell door and release a prisoner, as he'd been bribed to do. Then he and his wife took off with what must have been a rich reward, given that Tom must now be on the run, and without a job. Does that sound likely to you?'

'Yes, sir,' said Possett. 'Do you want to put the word out for him?'

'You mean you haven't *already*?' Edward yelled. 'And what about the prisoner he was supposed to be guarding — Robert Cropper?'

'We've put the word out for him, sir,' Possett said proudly.

'And have you also alerted the Town Sheriff's office? After all, if either of them is still in the town, it's a matter that falls within their jurisdiction.'

'I'll do that right away, sir,' Possett offered.

Edward nodded. 'Very well. But just notify the constables in the Guildhall, and leave it to me to speak with the town bailiff.'

Less than an hour later, Edward was drinking small beer with Francis at his house in Whitefriars Lane, and apologising for the additional work.

'Don't concern yourself, Edward,' said Francis. 'After the tumult of the past few days, the search for two missing men will seem like a day off.'

'Talking of days off,' Edward began, 'could I possibly prevail upon you to assume county duties for one day in the near future, assuming that Sir John will permit it? I still haven't met Elizabeth's parents, and she's beginning to press me about it.'

'Of course, provided that I might seek the same favour from you in return. There are days when I would like to be free to pursue certain interests of my own without wondering when I shall have to endure the next interruption. So what additional detail do you have regarding this escaped prisoner?'

'He's the burglar Robert Cropper — one of those awaiting trial at the next assize. But I am equally anxious to locate the missing turnkey Thomas Tapper, if only to make an example of him in case any others feel tempted to assist in the escape of a criminal. Given a little pressure, he may also be able to assist us in understanding why someone as lowly and closely confined as Cropper was able to finance his own escape.'

'Might this explain why two justices were murdered?' Francis asked. 'Were such acts committed to give Cropper time to flee?'

Edward shook his head. 'Cropper is only a common burglar, and by all accounts a not particularly successful or intelligent one. How could he come by either the money or the contacts to bring about such outrages?'

'Perhaps you are correct, but the coincidence is striking,' Francis conceded. At that moment, there was a commotion at his front door, and his houseboy ushered in a sweating constable.

'Pardon the intrusion, sir,' he said to Francis, 'but it's perhaps as well that the other bailiff's here as well — the one from the county — since I'm not sure which side of the boundary the body belongs to.'

'Body?' Francis echoed.

The man nodded. 'Yes, sirs. It's under one of the arches of Hethbeth Bridge, which means it might belong to one of you or the other, but we're not sure which.'

'Then perhaps we'd *both* better come along, Constable,' Francis suggested as he rose to his feet. 'Come with me, Edward. These past few days have been quite like old times, have they not?'

They rode hard across the town to its eastern approaches, urging their horses towards the bridge that spanned both the Leen and the Trent rivers.

It was obvious even from a distance that something brutal had taken place. There was dried blood all over the grass around the body, and the thin clothing had been ripped to shreds by sharp blades.

Edward looked hard at what was left. 'I believe this to have been Robert Cropper,' he advised Francis, 'in which case we needed no judge and jury to rid the county of a pest.'

'How can you be certain?' Francis enquired. 'And which of us is to claim the body?'

'It's definitely mine,' said Edward. 'He escaped from my custody while awaiting trial for offences in the county. As to my certainty, look at his clothing — threadbare, as befits one who has spent some time in a solitary cell underground, as does the paleness of his skin. And look at the scars on his back: they are old, a legacy of several whippings he received for previous crimes. Although I only saw Robert Cropper very briefly when he was brought in by the local constable following his latest capture, the sorry remains here are consistent with what I recall of his appearance.'

'But what sort of ironic misfortune leads to a man escaping a prison cell, and then encountering robbers within an hour of having done so?' Francis objected. 'He can hardly have presented a prospect of rich pickings to any bunch of cut-throats.'

'They were no mere cut-throats,' Edward observed as he nodded down at the corpse. 'Those are sword wounds — how many cut-throats are armed with swords rather than daggers? This was no chance encounter, either. Whoever set about him knew that he would be heading this way, and lay in wait for him.'

'You suggest that those who killed him were the same as those who organised his release?' Francis asked, totally bemused. 'Why would they have a man smuggled out of the gaol, only to murder him within the hour?'

Edward mulled over what they knew so far. 'Within the past week, two justices who were supposed to try cases at the local assize were brutally done to death. We thought that this was a prelude to a mass uprising against the established order, but we may now suppose that the deeds were committed simply to cause a delay in holding the assize.'

'For what purpose?'

'To allow time for Robert Cropper to be removed from his cell and done to death, I believe.'

'If they wanted him dead, why not simply arrange for your rogue turnkey to do the deed while Cropper was locked in a cell, and powerless to defend himself?'

'Because that would draw too much attention to the real reason for his planned death. They wished him to seem to be the victim of street robbers.'

'A man with no money, dressed in those gaol rags?'

'Well, perhaps it was meant instead to look like the aftermath of a simple street brawl.'

'Between an unarmed man and one or two sturdy villains armed with swords?'

'Do not seek to ascribe either logic or even common sense to what happened, Francis — simply observe that it happened. Someone was desperate to have Cropper silenced.'

'For what reason?'

'This I am unable to fathom, but my instinct tells me that it is connected with the reason why he was taken up by the local constable. Let us consult the paper locked in my desk at the Shire Hall, and give orders for Cropper's remains to be conveyed there. Then we may begin to seek some reason for this seemingly meaningless slaughter.'

A grinning Will Possett met them in the vestibule of the Shire Hall.

'They've found Tom Tapper, sirs,' the turnkey said. 'He's been locked in the same cell that he let Cropper escape from.'

'Excellent!' Edward said, beaming. 'We'll deal with him once we've taken some refreshment. Where was he found?'

'At Chapel Bar. He and his missus were trying to leave town for Lenton, where they've got family. We only brought him back — we let his missus go, because we know where to find her. Anyway, she hasn't done anything, as far as we know.'

After refreshing themselves with small beer and a pie from a street vendor along High Pavement, Edward and Francis descended two levels into the bowels of the Shire Hall to confront the man who had facilitated Cropper's escape. Tom Tapper sat resignedly in a dusty corner of the cell, and barely acknowledged their presence as they were admitted through the heavy oak door and stood looking down at him menacingly.

'I suppose I'll go on trial for murdering Rob Cropper,' Tapper muttered. 'But it wasn't me who did it.'

'We'd concluded that for ourselves,' Edward said. 'This gentleman with me is the town bailiff, Francis Barton, and he agrees that whoever killed Cropper was more skilled at it than you were likely to be. You seem to know, however, that he was destined for death once you allowed him to escape. But what you did was even more serious than murder: the appropriate charge would be "sedition" — rebellion against the established order.'

'You're going to put me on trial for that, then?' Tapper asked with seeming disinterest.

'Who said anything about a trial?' said Edward, watching Tapper's head jerk up in horror. 'We'll just take you out into the yard and string you up, then bury your body in the pit with the other hanged criminals. Only a few people know that you've been recaptured, so we'll just let it be thought that you made a successful escape.'

'You wouldn't!' Tapper protested. 'You've got too much respect for the law to do that!'

'We might,' Edward replied ominously. 'But that depends on how well you can make amends by telling us who put you up to it, and why.'

'It was some fancy bloke I owed money to,' Tapper muttered. 'Me and him played cards at the Black Swan, down on Malin Hill. I lost so much that the bastard threatened to slit my throat unless I either paid him what I owed or did him a small favour in letting someone out of the gaol. I didn't really have a choice.'

'Describe this man,' Francis demanded.

Tapper shrugged. 'Like I said, he was fancy — as if he were gentry or something. I'd never seen him before in the Black Swan. He just came up to where I was sitting in the back room, pulled out this pack of cards, and invited me to play a game called "primero", which I hadn't played before. After only a short while, I owed him more than I could pay back.'

'So he offered you a way out of your difficulty by demanding that you release Robert Cropper?' Edward persisted.

'That's right,' said Tapper. 'I was asked to take him from his cell and lead him out to the yard at the back, where I'd fixed a rope for him to drop down into Narrow Marsh below. I was to tell him to go with the man who'd be waiting for him at the bottom, and that he'd take him to a horse.'

'But you suspected that he was to be murdered?' Edward demanded angrily.

Tapper nodded. 'But he was going to be hung anyway, wasn't he?'

'That was to depend upon the outcome of his trial,' Edward reminded him sternly. 'A trial that was delayed because of the murder of two justices in quick succession. You're lucky that you weren't murdered yourself, since this crew of villains don't hesitate to butcher anyone who gets in their way. Your colleague Joe Bilthorpe certainly had a lucky escape, with only a case of the flux to keep him away from his duties that night. Perhaps we should just release you, then let it be known that you betrayed the identities of those who murdered Robert Cropper. You wouldn't remain alive for another hour, I'd imagine.'

'No — please!' Tapper pleaded. 'I'll take my chances at trial, but don't do *that* to me!'

'Then tell us more about the man you played cards with,' said Edward.

Tapper screwed up his face in heavy concentration as he tried to recall the man's appearance. 'I didn't really see his face, because he was wearing this big hat with a wide brim that came down right over his nose. But he talked all high and mighty, like real gentry, and he told me he was one of those players that goes round the country, performing for the rich in their country houses. That's about all I can tell you, I'm afraid.'

'That may be enough,' Edward replied with a grim smile, 'since it matches other information in our possession. Enjoy your stay here, Tapper, which may well be a long one, until we can find a justice courageous enough to come to Nottingham.'

Back upstairs in Edward's modest chamber, Francis reminded him that he had promised to reveal further information about Cropper's arrest. Edward unlocked his desk, extracted a piece of vellum and sat down opposite Francis.

'Here we are,' he said. 'A list of the things that Cropper stole from that manor house in Cotgrave — the Lacey house. Let's see: the usual things, such as silver plate, a candle holder, a statue of the Virgin, and — oh dear God, I was right!'

'What?' Francis demanded.

Edward dropped the vellum onto his desk with a triumphant smile. 'I *knew* that we were not battling coincidence. One of the items that Cropper stole was a crossbow!'

7

'Why doesn't your employer's guest wish you to be invited to supper?' Elizabeth asked. She was annoyed by the seeming slight to Edward as she watched Holles's distinguished guest, Baron Burghley, being assisted down from his coach at the grand entrance to Thurland Hall. The household had been awaiting his arrival for several days, and a footman had been outside for the past hour, looking out for his coach.

'It was Sir John's decision, not Baron Burghley's,' Edward advised her. 'When the latter learns my true identity, he will no doubt wish to have me taken out and horse-whipped.'

'Why so? Is he not Her Majesty's closest adviser? And was she not greatly impressed by your efforts in preventing her image being besmirched at the Scottish court? I still cannot believe her idiot envoy faced no punishment for abducting prostitutes and trying to gift them to the Scottish king in Her Majesty's name! It's fortunate that you caught up with him before he handed the women over.'

Edward laughed. 'You have clearly forgotten who that "idiot envoy" was: Robert Cecil was the man behind the heinous plan. The old man you see outside is his father; before he was Baron Burghley, he was merely Sir William Cecil.'

'How can such a wise and respected counsellor have such a stupid son?'

'That is no doubt a question which he asks himself daily,' said Edward with a grin. 'But blood ties are strong. I am assured by Sir John that Baron Burghley wishes to speak with both myself and Francis regarding the recent outrages in both our jurisdictions. Before we meet, he must be gently advised that I am the man who thwarted his son.'

Robert Cecil had shifted the blame for the abductions onto the men in his employment, insisting that he knew nothing about the plan. He had thus avoided the worst of the queen's wrath. However, the Earl of Essex, who had helped Edward to rescue the prostitutes, knew the full extent of Cecil's involvement. Essex had decided not to reveal what he knew unless or until he could do so to his own advantage. Since both men were rivals for the queen's favour, this put Cecil in a precarious position at court.

'If Burghley does not go off like a Tower cannon when he learns my identity, I shall be invited to speak with him after he has been lulled with wine and a fine supper.'

'And Francis?'

'It has been agreed that he and Edmund Jowett will join us on the morrow. Seemingly Burghley's first message is for my ears only; at least, that is the instruction that was sent north ahead of his lordship's arrival.'

'So you are free to take supper here with me?'

'I am indeed, so where is it?'

'Meg was required to visit her mother in Basford earlier today, so she is a little behind with everything. But supper should be served within the hour. Perhaps you might wish to use the time to change your attire, in order to present a finer sight than you do at present.'

Two hours later a refreshed and recently fed Edward was summoned by an attendant into the main residential wing of Thurland Hall. He was then ushered into the great hall, in which Sir John Holles and his distinguished guest sat on either side of a blazing fire. A slightly nervous-looking Sir John rose and welcomed Edward, then instructed the server to bring another goblet for their new arrival and pour him some wine. Then he effected the introductions.

'Baron Burghley, allow me to introduce the county bailiff, Edward Mountsorrel. I don't believe that you and he have met before.'

'Indeed we have not,' Burghley replied with a stern face, 'although he and my son Robert became well acquainted some months ago, when your man stubbornly interfered in matters of state that were no business of his.'

'I was not seeking to deal with matters of state, my lord,' Edward replied coolly as he bowed his head to the minimum degree required by protocol. 'I was simply performing my duty in rescuing five young women from a life of sexual slavery at a foreign court. It was fortunate that the man who had planned the abductions was so dull-witted that he had not foreseen that someone might come in search of them.'

Holles inhaled sharply, and for a moment Burghley seemed taken aback by the effrontery. Then a smile spread across his countenance.

'You would indeed appear to be as stubborn and foolhardy as Robert described. But these are qualities that you may need in abundance if you are to fulfil the role that your nation requires that you undertake.'

'Is that why I am summoned here, my lord?' Edward enquired. 'If so, you will not find me wanting.'

'That remains to be seen,' Burghley replied as his face clouded over, 'but before we discuss that, let me give you a friendly warning against ever again seeking the support of the Earl of Essex. Robert Devereux grows too cocky for his own good these days, and it is only a matter of time before he overreaches himself and falls out of Her Majesty's favour.'

'I thank you for that advice, my lord,' Edward replied stiffly, fully aware of the rivalry at court between Essex and the Cecils.

Holles bid Edward take the vacant chair in front of the fire. 'Please pay close attention to what Baron Burghley has to impart,' he instructed him.

The old man cleared the phlegm from his throat, took another sip of wine, and began. 'You are of course aware that Her Majesty currently remains unmarried, and has now reached an age at which she is unlikely to give birth?' When Edward remained silent, the old man pressed on. 'That being the case, the question naturally arises as to who shall be named as her heir. She has proved resistant to naming anyone, despite my entreaties and those of her entire Privy Council. If she dies without declaring the succession, then there are but two possible blood claimants.'

'One of whom is the current King of Scotland,' Edward put in, having learned this from his previous dealings with the Earl of Essex. 'And I believe that the other is a woman who is also a royal cousin of sorts.'

'This will be easier than I had feared,' said Burghley, 'although I tremble to think what garbled nonsense Essex gave you regarding the validity of each of their claims.'

'On that point he was silent,' Edward said diplomatically.

'Then he was very wise,' said Burghley. 'But let me add some background, because therein lies the danger that the nation currently faces, in the way of civil war.'

The mention of war grabbed Edward's attention, and he leaned in to listen.

'I must begin by reminding you of what a complex family the Tudors have proved to be. I ask your forgiveness, but it is the only way for you to understand why the nation is currently poised upon a sword edge. The first of the Tudors — Henry, the seventh of that name — had three children who survived him. One, of course, was the late King Henry who fathered Elizabeth, our current queen. But Henry had two sisters, the younger of whom, Mary, was the progenitor of the Grey family that produced the Lady Jane, of whom we need say no more. I trust that I still have your attention?'

'Indeed,' said Edward, 'since I once worked on the estate of another branch of the Grey family.'

'That is not a matter that should be openly boasted about in Tudor circles. Allow me to continue, since it is the older sister of the late King Henry whose fortunes we must follow. She was named Margaret, and her first husband was the King of Scotland, James IV. Her granddaughter through that line was the Mary of Scotland whom Her Majesty was obliged to have executed in recent years because of the Catholic threat that she posed to the throne of England. She was, of course, a cousin of sorts to our queen.'

'And this Mary was the mother of the current King of Scotland?' Edward prompted him.

'Indeed. Her marriage to her second husband, Lord Darnley, resulted in the birth of James of Scotland, the current ruler of that nation and the first of the two claimants to the throne should Her Majesty die.'

'As indeed she must, one day,' Edward mused. He received a stern frown from Burghley and a warning glare from Holles.

'It is not wise to mention death in the same sentence as the monarch, since it is so easily misconstrued as treasonous,' Burghley warned, before continuing his explanations. 'Aside from James, there is another claimant of equal standing.'

It fell silent for a moment, the only sound being that of a log slipping to the front of the fireplace.

'Margaret Tudor married again, following the death of her first husband James of Scotland,' Burghley went on. 'This second marriage was to Archibald Douglas, Earl of Angus, and it produced a daughter, Lady Margaret Douglas. She in turn married Matthew Stuart, Earl of Lennox, and had two sons, the elder of whom was Lord Darnley — now deceased, of course. I see your eyes beginning to glaze over — should I repeat any of that?'

'No, simply let me absorb it for a moment,' Edward requested. 'It would seem that the claim the current King of Scotland has to the English throne comes from his grandmother having been a sister of Henry VIII, which makes the original Henry Tudor his great-grandfather.'

'You have the nub of it,' Burghley confirmed. 'But remember what I said about the line of descent from Margaret Tudor? Lord Darnley's younger brother Charles married Elizabeth Cavendish, and they had a daughter called Arbella Stuart, who currently resides but a day's ride north of here, in Derbyshire. She is related to our current queen in almost the same degree as James of Scotland, and therefore she has a claim to the throne of England.'

Edward thought carefully. 'But she is a woman. It might be thought by some that since England has had two queens in succession, this time the people might prefer a king.'

Burghley chuckled. 'I do not recommend that you make that suggestion to Her Majesty, given her frequent assertions that the nation has fared well under her protection. That way lies the Tower.'

'I meant no disrespect to Her Majesty,' Edward hastened to assure him. 'It is simply the fact that the people seek a strong leader and protector, and that by tradition we have been led by warrior kings. That said, I was at Tilbury with the Earl of

Leicester when Her Majesty gave a stirring speech that left us all inspired to take on the Spanish.'

'Her Majesty has certainly inherited her father's fire,' Burghley replied with a smile that faded almost immediately. 'Her Council fear to open their mouths in the wrong direction, since her wrath is terrible to behold — and I speak as someone who has known her since she was a frightened young girl, during the reign of her half-sister Mary. None dare speak of the succession, lest it be taken as an observation that she is fading with the years.'

'Has she given no indication of which of the claimants has her favour?' Edward asked.

'No, which obliges us in Council to think about what is best for England once she has passed on. For your ears only, I will say that it is feared that this will come sooner rather than later, given the frequency of her illnesses.'

'And what does the Council conclude?'

Burghley sighed. 'It is a question well asked. As has been the case in this nation for the past thirty years and more, it is a matter of religion.'

'The two claimants have opposing views on how one should worship God, you mean?' Edward asked.

'Yes and no.' Burghley lowered his voice. 'We now reach the point where I must ask you to be circumspect regarding our conversation, and preferably to forget that it ever took place at all. One word of what I have to say to anyone outside this room, and I will know where to send the Tower escort. We are *ad idem* on that?'

Both Edward and Holles nodded eagerly, and Burghley gazed up at the ceiling as he continued.

'We may begin with King James, who everyone believes to embrace the Protestant faith. The same faith that Elizabeth has promoted, to her considerable cost over the years. James's mother was of course a fervent and unrepentant Catholic, and it was a succession of her Catholic devotees who promoted several uprisings against the throne which led to the need to have her executed. This in turn provoked Elizabeth's excommunication by the Pope, and his support for the attempted Spanish invasion. So Her Majesty is clearly set against any resumption of the old religion in this country, and one might therefore anticipate her preference for James's claim.'

'Do I suspect correctly that there is a "but" about to be delivered?' Edward enquired.

Burghley frowned. 'You are indeed swift on the uptake, Master Mountsorrel. James is known to have opinions regarding the role of the monarch in the management of the national religion that made some of Her Majesty's Council fear that if he becomes king, he will seek to impose whatever religious view he privately holds as the nation's religion. In short, that he will become the head of the Church as well as the State, ruling absolutely in both.'

'Is that not, in reality, what Her Majesty has also done?' Edward asked. He knew nothing about religion; he had turned his back on it many years previously.

Burghley's reaction was one of shocked anger. 'Whence comes that notion? Is that some offal put into your brain by the dissembler Essex? A man who is rumoured to surround himself with Catholics in order to strengthen his following? I was present in person at an early meeting of Elizabeth's Council when they begged her to assume the role of head of the Church of England — "Defender of the Faith", as her father had so proclaimed himself. She demurred, consenting only to be styled "Governor" of the Church, rather than its

"Head", which she thought smacked too much of a divine ordination. She has always sought to allow men to worship according to their conscience, and we have so far kept from her the knowledge that her possible successor would rule the kingdom bequeathed to him rather as the Emperors of Rome once ruled as gods in their own right.'

'You have kept this knowledge from her so as not to blight James's cause?' Edward asked bluntly. During his previous clash with Robert Cecil, Edward had formed the distinct impression that the Master Secretary and his son were backing the Scots King's claim in the hope that their loyalty to his cause would be amply rewarded with high office upon his accession.

Burghley frowned. 'You presume too far, young man. My concern has ever been to uphold the Queen's Peace throughout her realm, as it is your sworn duty to maintain it in Nottinghamshire. My fear, and that of the Council, is that England will be too easily exposed to her Catholic enemies overseas should there be no rapid succession by a strong Protestant. At present, James is our best hope in that regard.'

'The other claimant?' Edward persevered. 'The woman who is yet but a girl? Apart from the her age, is she also Catholic in her beliefs?'

'So it is strongly believed,' Burghley replied. 'I have already revealed her to be Arbella Stuart, cousin to James and cousin through the second degree to Elizabeth. She has so far evinced no desire to become queen, although she is surrounded by those who prevail upon her to think in such grandiose terms. Chief among these is her grandmother, one of the wealthiest and best connected ladies in England.'

'Her name?' Edward prompted him.

'Elizabeth Cavendish, on whose Derbyshire estate of Chatsworth Arbella has been raised, and under whose influence she has increasingly fallen since the deaths of both her parents. She is referred to as "Bess", to distinguish her from her daughter of the same name, Arbella's mother. For the past few years, Bess has been married to Sir George Talbot, Earl of Shrewsbury.'

'He I have met!' said Edward. 'He was our host in more than one establishment when Essex and I rode north in pursuit of your son and his captive prostitutes.'

A flash of anger lit Burghley's countenance, but he nodded. 'It would have been difficult not to rely on the hospitality of Talbot on any journey north of the Trent, since he owns most of the estates to be found there. So many, in fact, that when Elizabeth was seeking somewhere to safely house the Scots Mary under the supervision of a trusted gaoler, he was the obvious choice. When I advise you that one of those safe prisons was Chatsworth itself, you may perhaps deduce where this conversation might be heading.'

When Edward failed to voice any connections that might have clicked inside his head, Burghley continued.

'Bess Cavendish — or Bess Talbot, as we should perhaps call her — is an accomplished needlewoman, and the Scots Mary was known to while away her solitary hours in needlework of her own. It was perhaps inevitable that the two women should end up spending many hours in each other's company, picking at their needlepoint and exchanging family tittle-tattle. If you recall what I told you earlier, Bess was mother-in-law to the brother of Lord Darnley, which meant that they were directly related by marriage. It is believed that on many of these afternoons, the two women were joined by Bess's granddaughter Arbella, to whom Mary gave instruction on her heritage, and how to behave as a queen.'

'But this is pure conjecture?' Edward asked.

Burghley gave a cynical snort. 'At present, it's little more than that. But consider it this way: when Arbella's mother died some eight years ago, when the girl was merely seven years of age, her wardship should have fallen to me, as Master of the Court of Wards. But Her Majesty advised me that this was not necessary, and that it had been agreed that Arbella was to fall under the wardship of her grandmother Bess. This was said to be because Bess had learned the ways of courtly life while attending as a lady-in-waiting to Anne Gainsford, Lady Zouche, who in turn was lady-in-waiting to Elizabeth's mother when she was merely Anne Boleyn, and not Queen of England.'

'My wife was raised on the Zouche estate!' Edward blurted out without thinking. 'Her father was its steward, and her mother its housekeeper.'

'This is perhaps all to the good,' Burghley smiled, 'since it will be necessary for you to acquire such knowledge as you can of who now attends upon Arbella, and what their business may be.'

'If she is staunchly Catholic, as is implied by what you have told me already,' Edward hedged, 'then why is she still being regarded as a claimant to Elizabeth's Protestant throne?'

Burghley sighed. 'Perhaps you are not so attuned to matters of political reality as I had begun to hope. Her claim to the throne comes only from the dice throw of her birth. If she is Catholic, then she should perhaps be thought of no further as the potential future Queen of England. But in her may lie all the frustrated hopes and ambitions of Catholics throughout the realm, and she may become as much an inspiration for rebellion as ever the Scots Mary was.'

'And it is this that you wish to prevent?'

'It is more than that, Master Mountsorrel. I wish to strangle it at birth, and I believe that the events here in Nottinghamshire in recent weeks are the first pains of that birth.'

'So what do you wish of me?' Edward enquired. His blood stirred at the prospect of the sort of action for which he had once been trained.

Burghley shook his head and nodded towards the glowing embers in the fireplace. 'The night draws on, and I am weary after travelling. But more to the point, what I have to further disclose must be in the presence of the peacekeepers of the town as well as the county, so that I am not called upon to repeat myself. And so until the morrow.'

8

The next day, once Holles's guests were gathered in the ground-floor chamber, the Thurland Hall steward backed out of the room. He passed on the instruction to the footman that he was to remain at his post in the rear corridor, ensuring that no-one either entered that chamber or remained close enough to the door to overhear the conversation inside it.

There were five of them around the table that had been loaded with small beer and wafers to sustain them until dinner, which would not be served until Holles gave the order. He had given pride of place at the head of the table to Baron Burghley, and down one side of it sat Holles and Edward, with Francis Barton and Edmund Jowett, Sheriff of Nottingham, down the other side. The atmosphere was made even more tense by the strained look on Burghley's face as he braced himself to disclose information that not even Her Majesty was privy to at this stage.

'Have any of you ever heard of "The Brotherhood of the Blood of Christ"?' he asked. When he had counted four heads being shaken, he continued, 'This is perhaps as well, but I must swear each of you to an oath of secrecy regarding both its name and its very existence. But what image does the mere name summon in your minds?'

'The Knights Templar,' Edward responded.

Francis went pale as he answered, 'A group of staunch Catholics sworn to avenge the crucifixion of Christ.'

Burghley nodded. 'And you would both be correct, each of you in your own way. They are, in fact, dedicated to the restoration of the Catholic faith in England.'

'They actually exist?' Holles gasped.

'They do indeed, and they have been active in England for the best part of a year.'

'Your answer suggests that they originate from elsewhere,' Edward commented.

'They're from France and Italy, in the main,' said Burghley. 'When Elizabeth succeeded to the throne, dedicated to reviving the Protestant movement begun by her father, many Catholics who had prospered during the reign of Mary fled to the Continent, fearing persecution. To Her Majesty's great credit, and in accordance with advice that I and others urged upon her, there was no such persecution. However, as the recent history of our realm has shown, there is no shortage of those of the old faith who are determined to see England handed back to Rome.'

'Such as the Scots Mary and those who prevailed upon her to stir up rebellion and plots against the throne?' Edward offered.

'That's right. Whence came those treasonous influences, say you?' Burghley enquired, looking at those around the table. The men's blank expressions encouraged him to continue. 'Almost immediately after the first Catholic exiles made their way across the Channel, the universities of France and Italy began providing for their needs. There was soon a network of what became known as "English Colleges" that were dedicated to the training of priests who could be sent back to England in order to keep the flame of Catholicism alive among the old families with large estates and Popish loyalties.'

As he paused to moisten his throat with a mouthful of small beer, Holles made his own contribution.

'Some of those estates may be found here in Nottinghamshire, may they not? I have heard whispers of Masses being conducted in secret by priests smuggled into the country houses. It is said that they were hidden behind the wainscoting when inquisitors came calling, sent by Sir Francis Walsingham. His death last year must have come as a great blow to Her Majesty.'

'Indeed,' Burghley agreed with a solemn countenance. 'But the spymaster's death must not be allowed to diminish our efforts in hunting down these blasphemous and treasonous rats that scuttle behind the framework of the English edifice.' Conscious that his imagery had perhaps grown too vivid for his audience, he resumed his original theme.

'These English Colleges continue to thrive, and they produce a large supply of priests who cross the Channel by night, and are harboured on country estates. We are in danger of losing the battle to stem the flow. And it has now become more perilous, since some of their number have been trained, equipped, and financed to instigate physical rebellion. In short, gentleman, England is in great danger of being overrun by Catholic zealots who will stop at nothing — not even the removal of Her Majesty — to serve the will of the Pope, and, in their own misguided belief, to secure their souls a place in Heaven.'

'These are "The Brotherhood" to whom you referred earlier?' Edward put in.

'Indeed,' said Burghley. '"The Brotherhood of the Blood of Christ" was, we believe, formed over a year ago, when a Jesuit priest called Robert Southwell was sent here by the English College in Rome, in the company of a fellow fanatic called Henry Garnet. We believe that their mission was to form a military arm of the covert Catholic community that was lurking behind the woodwork — one that would rise up and replace Elizabeth with a surviving descendant of Tudor blood who was of their faith, and had been covertly prepared to don the crown of England.'

'She whose identity was revealed to me yesterday?' Edward enquired.

Burghley smiled. 'Indeed she, and I am gratified that our meeting by the fireside after supper was not in vain. I shall leave it to you to advise your colleague Master Barton here of the girl's identity, and move on to explain my purpose for being here in Nottingham.'

The silence was palpable as Burghley looked slowly round at each of their faces in turn.

'We believe that the recent murders of the two justices were ordered by whoever commands the local contingent of the Brotherhood.'

'They have more than one armed band?' Edward asked, both aghast and curious to learn how an entire army could remain undetected. Then he recalled the incident just north of Costock and asked, 'Does this local leader have a flair for the dramatic, by any chance?'

'If he is who we believe him to be, then almost certainly,' Burghley confirmed. 'Why do you ask?'

'Well, the band of four who killed Justice Mortley just outside Costock would seem to have changed their apparel just before they committed the deed. They had given the impression that they were country gentlemen while staying at a local inn the previous night. Then they donned costumes for the outrage itself that made them resemble a band of ragged cut-throats.'

'Very appropriate, given that Nottinghamshire was once the home of the most famous outlaw of them all — Robin Hood,' said Burghley.

'There is no reason to believe that he ever existed,' Sheriff Jowett objected. 'And there was no Sheriff of Nottingham in those days. My office is barely a hundred years old.'

'Precisely,' Burghley agreed. 'A perfect subject for rural myth, and one that would appeal to the man we believe to be both giving and taking orders in this part of the country.'

'Who might he be?' Edward pressed.

'His name is Christopher Marlowe,' Burghley revealed, 'and he passes himself off as a writer of masques and extended mummeries. Theatres are increasingly popular in London, where such performances may be staged in return for payment. But for those who live outside London, the only way to enjoy such distractions is to invite the players to perform them in the main hall of a country mansion. What could be a more convenient means of disguising a band of assassins than to have them masquerade as travelling players, moving from one wealthy estate to another?'

'What makes you believe that this man Marlowe may be anything other than what he purports to be?' asked Holles.

Burghley inclined his head. 'You will recall our conversation yesterday, when I made reference to a certain young lady of Catholic persuasion who resides not a half day's ride from here, at Chatsworth? The ward of Bess Talbot?'

'May we not name her?' Edward enquired. 'I can vouch for my colleague and friend Francis Barton, and if one cannot share a confidence with his employer the Sheriff of Nottingham, then perhaps this conversation ought not to be taking place at all.'

'Very well,' Burghley conceded as he half turned in his chair to address Francis and Jowett. 'Her name is Arbella Stuart, and she is a potential successor to Queen Elizabeth. However, she is Catholic in her beliefs, and easily manipulated by those who would seek to use her as a puppet monarch in order to ensure that England is once again in thrall to Rome.'

'And what of her possible connection with this man Marlowe?' Edward persisted.

'He is believed to have ministered to her as her tutor during her early years under the wardship of her grandmother,' Burghley replied with a broad smile.

'And you believe this Marlowe to have been behind the death of Justices Mortley and Brigham?' Edward persevered.

'That is the case, and from what you tell me about the circumstances surrounding the first of those murders, it has all the hallmarks of a carefully conceived theatrical performance. It was a real-life tragedy of the style in which Marlowe is known to indulge.'

'What is known of Marlowe's religious beliefs?' Francis asked, unsure whether to believe any of this.

'He was once a student of Cambridge University, from which he disappeared mysteriously during his final year of study. It is believed that the reason for his absence was his conversion to Catholicism and his desire to be trained, then ordained, as a priest. According to what my old friend and fellow priest-hunter Francis Walsingham was able to learn through his former network of spies, Marlowe was diverted from his priestly ambitions and recruited instead to act as a captain to one group of a larger company of brigands for Rome. He may even have received this commission directly from the hand of the Pope, because he is known to have been associated with the English College there, known as the "Collegio Romano".'

'I have evidence of it!' Edward shouted triumphantly. 'It is at my lodgings just across the courtyard. If I might be permitted to bring it in here?'

Burghley nodded, but reminded Edward that he was to disclose nothing of what had been discussed between them. As Edward hurried from the room, it was Francis's turn to seek answers.

'Edward and I have been pondering the reason why two justices were murdered in such quick succession. We concluded that it was either an attack on our justice system generally, or something specific to the assize that was slated to be held here in Nottingham. Can you add anything that would assist our ruminations?'

'Surely, had it been the former,' Burghley reasoned, 'then there would have been other attacks, on other justices, and in respect of other assizes. So it must have been something that was in danger of being revealed during one of the trials scheduled for your assize.'

'There *was* something else, as Edward can reveal upon his return,' Francis confided. 'A man who was due to stand trial at that assize — a common burglar called Cropper — was allowed to escape from his cell for long enough for him to be done to death in a dark place near the river. It is Edward's belief that the reason for this was to do with something he had stolen from a country house — a crossbow. Why that might be significant he has yet to reveal to me, but he can explain it to you himself.'

While he'd been talking Edward had returned to the room, clearly animated and in a hurry. Beads of sweat were forming on his forehead just below the brim of his bonnet, and he was out of breath. In his hand was an ornately bound prayer book, which he eagerly handed to Burghley.

'I found this at the scene of the attack on Justice Mortley. I believe it to have been left behind by those responsible. As you can see, the inner cover has some sort of dedication from the

"Collegio Romano" that you mentioned, and it names the person who must have lost it in his anxiety to depart the place where he had just taken part in the murders!'

Burghley read the dedication that had been pasted inside the front cover. 'You are correct. According to the Latin inscription, it was presented to someone known as "Richard of Lincoln" on the day of his ordination. This seems to confirm our belief that those who have been striking blows at our justice system have been sent here as warrior priests from one of the English Colleges of which I spoke. As for identifying who once owned it, we know only that he was called "Richard", and that he came originally from Lincoln. But that may not be his birth name.'

'So it does not assist us?' Edward asked, crestfallen.

'It does, of course, in that it confirms the motives of those responsible,' Burghley hastened to reassure him.

'While you were out of the room, I mentioned the crossbow that Cropper had stolen from the house in Cotgrave,' Francis advised Edward.

'Well remembered,' Edward nodded, the light of enthusiasm still glowing in his eyes. 'It seemed to me to be a strange thing for a common burglar to steal, but I believe that this was what got him murdered. The crossbow revealed something regarding the actions of those residing in the house. It is on an estate in Cotgrave belonging to the Lacey family, who are leading landholders in these parts. It lies in the same part of the county as Costock, south of the town, and less than half a day's ride from there.'

'But what is the significance of such an ancient piece of weaponry?' Burghley asked.

'The murders at Costock were committed with crossbows — or at least, most of them were!' Edward explained. 'This surely defies coincidence?'

'Indeed it does,' Burghley agreed, 'and it further confirms that these deluded followers of the Roman way are being harboured in the country houses of those who share their old faith, as they travel the countryside posing as strolling players. It therefore suits the plan that I have devised, and which is the reason for my visit here.'

'You wish us to go in pursuit of these evil-doers?' Francis enquired eagerly. 'Smoke them like rats from grain stores?'

'In essence, yes,' Burghley confirmed, 'but not by laying siege to their hiding places, or riding onto country estates with an army of men-at-arms. They are too well protected, and most of them seemingly skilled in the art of warfare. Your approach must therefore be a more subtle one.'

'What have you in mind?' Edward asked.

Burghley folded his hands across his chest. 'For you, a role that should come easily. I wish you to resume your status as a former soldier of fortune fallen upon hard times. You served under Leicester at Tilbury, but like so many of those discharged from Her Majesty's service following the defeat of the Armada, you have been wandering the nation ever since, in search of the means of earning your livelihood. Now it has occurred to you that you might have a future as a travelling player, given your physical prowess, your commanding voice and your martial bearing. You will present yourself to Master Marlowe in that capacity, and he will hopefully encourage you to join his band with a view to recruiting you into his murderous coterie of traitors. I have been watching you carefully these past two days, and I believe that you can play the part to perfection.'

'But surely there is a risk that I will be recognised by someone as the local bailiff?' Edward reasoned.

'In Nottinghamshire, certainly,' Burghley agreed. 'But not in Leicestershire, where it is believed that Marlowe and his followers are currently laying low, nor in Derbyshire, where they may be heading, and wherein may be found the Chatsworth estate on which Arbella Stuart resides.'

'I spent my early years in Leicestershire,' Edward said, 'although I left it as a member of its Trained Band, headed for service under Robert Dudley, so this would accord well with the pretended role that you now wish me to adopt. My wife is also from the same county, where she was trained in service as a lady's maid. May I take her with me?'

'Not only may you do so, but I think it would be all to the good,' Burghley agreed, 'since your ruse may be more convincing with two people who are familiar with the area.'

'What about Master Barton?' Edward asked, with a nod towards Francis. 'Is he to play the role of my servant?'

'It would not be realistic for a soldier reduced in fortune to have a servant trotting at his heels. Besides which, I have an important role for him also: I wish him to act as your messenger. Should you succeed in learning the true nature of Marlowe's business, and that of his entourage, you are to communicate this to Francis, who in turn will ride hard to Nottingham. The castle garrison has been recently strengthened with a company of hardened fighting men recruited from the Tower. They have been told to hold themselves in readiness for orders to close in on Marlowe's company and arrest them for treason.'

'And where will I post myself in readiness to receive that word from Edward?' Francis enquired.

'Wherever you deem it most appropriate,' Burghley replied. 'I shall leave coin with Master Jowett here, in order that you may install yourself at some inn close to wherever Edward may be, there to receive his messages. You may pose as a travelling merchant or some such.'

'How will I get word to Francis from whichever mansion I may be installed in?' Edward asked.

Burghley shrugged. 'That will be for you to decide, but perhaps it would be less suspicious for your wife to slip away. She could claim to be visiting her family, since she once resided in the county.'

'Where within the county of Leicestershire may Marlowe currently be found?' Edward enquired.

'A place called Quorndon, at Nether Hall, the estate of the Farnham family,' Burghley replied. 'The head of that family, Sir Ralph, has long been suspect in his loyalties. Quorndon lies on the track that runs between Derby and Leicester.' He paused when he saw Edward's face fall. 'You would seem to already know of the place, and to judge by your expression, it does not meet with your approval.'

'I certainly know of it,' Edward said with a grimace, 'since it is less than an hour's ride north of the village of Mountsorrel, from where I take my name. It was the village in which I was abandoned by my mother shortly after my birth. She left me to the mercy of a kindly clergyman who had me conveyed to the orphanage in the hospital at Wigston, on the outskirts of Leicester. For reasons which I hope are obvious, I have avoided the place ever since.'

'But you are not known in Quorndon itself?'

'Not unless there are those there who remember an orphan boy who went on to work the land on the Grey estate at Groby.'

'But even should there be such persons, surely they would remember you merely as one who went to fight the Spanish? There are none who know of your current role as bailiff to the Sheriff of Nottinghamshire?'

'None of whom I am aware,' Edward replied cautiously. 'When I came to Nottingham, I did so directly from where we had encamped near Northampton following the retreat of the Armada. It was from there that the Earl of Leicester sent me north with a letter of commendation to the sheriff.'

'Then it is agreed, and it is almost dinner time,' Burghley concluded. 'Perhaps, Master Mountsorrel, you might wish to rejoin your wife, and give her the glad tidings regarding your orders for your immediate future.'

9

'Why the sudden change of heart?' Elizabeth enquired suspiciously after Edward gave her the news. 'You have always insisted that the pressure of your duties prevents us from making the long overdue visit for you to meet my parents for the first time, and now — when you and Francis are investigating so many wicked acts in such a short period of time — you are able to make the journey. How is this?'

'I am required by no less a person that the queen's secretary to journey down to a place in Leicestershire called Quorndon. There we will further our investigations into recent events which Burghley believes may be treasonous, and for this mission it is preferable that I be accompanied by my wife. Francis will be journeying with us, but he will leave us and ride on ahead when we reach Ashby. This would therefore provide the perfect opportunity for me to be introduced to your mother and father, who will hopefully conclude that their precious daughter has made a suitable match.'

'I get the strong feeling that I am not being given the entire reason, and I hope that this does not prove to be the start of a distance between us that you will blame upon your oath of office and the need for discretion. But I cannot deny that I have long anticipated the day when I can proudly lead you forward to meet Mother and Father.'

'Then it is decided,' Edward smiled encouragingly. 'When can you be ready for travel?'

'I am now even more suspicious,' Elizabeth frowned. 'You have always prevaricated regarding a journey to Ashby, even though it lies only half a day's ride south of here, but now that you have been given some special mission by Baron Burghley, you are impatient to leave. What is the purpose of this proposed visit to Quorndon, and where exactly shall we be staying?'

'The place is called Nether Hall, and it is on the estate of Sir Ralph Farnham. There Burghley has asked me to meet with a man called Christopher Marlowe, who is suspected of plotting against the Crown. He hides his true intentions behind a pretence of being a writer of dramas who is leading a group of travelling players. My mission is to pose as a discharged soldier down on his luck who is seeking to join the troupe.'

'A character not unlike your real self,' Elizabeth observed tartly as she rose from her chair by the window. 'And I am simply to play the role of your wife? Or did you have something more challenging for me, such as pretending that I'm a renegade nun escaping from convent vows, or perhaps a headstrong and ungrateful younger daughter seeking to evade an unwanted marriage being forced upon me by a wicked father?'

'Perhaps you should have been a playwright yourself,' Edward said with a grin, 'but for the present it will be sufficient for you to play the role of my wife — which you already do admirably, I may say.'

'Enough of the flattery, and get your boots off that chest — I need to open it to retrieve my travelling cloak. And I will need to instruct Meg to wash several gowns before we can even consider leaving.'

Three days later, Edward, Elizabeth and Francis were riding slowly along the approach to Kegworth village. The early summer dust clung to their faces and made them sneeze.

'May we call in at an inn for something to moisten our throats?' Elizabeth asked in a tone of voice that demanded an affirmative response.

Shortly afterwards they were seated at a table, watching children playing with a small dog on the village green. Francis took a long swig from his pot, then belched discreetly.

'This will soon be my daily activity,' he smiled, 'as I pose as a wealthy merchant, awaiting news from the newly appointed player in a humble company.'

'At least you were allocated a role that closely accords with your natural humour,' Edward complained. 'Had I wished to test my skills as one who stands before others and proclaims bad verse, I would not have joined the Leicestershire Trained Band. I'm a soldier at heart, not a performer of masques.'

'Will you be employing your real name?' Francis asked.

Edward shrugged. 'I have been giving that some thought, and on balance I believe that I should at least adopt an assumed second name. "Edward" may remain, since it is the name by which I have always been known, and it will be easier for Elizabeth to remember, so that she will not slip up when addressing me. As for my second name, I thought perhaps "Marshall", since it has a military ring to it. What think you, Francis — do I look like an "Edward Marshall"?'

Before Francis could reply, Elizabeth raised an objection.

'This makes me "Elizabeth Marshall", does it not? Did you not think to ask my opinion?' Before Edward could think of a suitable response, she went on, 'Francis, has Edward also sought to involve you in a matter that comes directly from the queen's secretary?'

'Burghley gave me my instructions directly,' Francis replied evasively, 'and they are simply to bide at a local inn when we reach Quorndon, there to await a message from Edward that I am to return to Nottingham with all speed.'

'And why might you be called upon to do that?' Elizabeth demanded. 'And for that matter, how will you receive such a message, if Edward is confined to the manor house of the local lord, pretending to be a mummer?'

When both men looked guiltily down at the table, Elizabeth's suspicion was confirmed.

'I am to be that messenger, am I not? That is the sole reason why you have brought me along, the pair of you — not because Edward desires me by his side, but because I am to act as a passer of information from one to the other. Admit it — is that not the case?'

'It is,' Edward admitted, then hastened to correct himself. 'I did wish you to be by my side, I assure you, but when it was agreed that you might accompany me, it occurred to us both that you would be the ideal person to slip from the manor house to the inn without alerting suspicion.'

'Except the suspicion that I might be a prostitute servicing travellers at the inn, of course!' Elizabeth replied hotly. 'Is that the *true* role that you both had in mind for me? If so, speak truthfully now, while there is still time for me to point my horse's head back in the direction from whence we came.'

'You should perhaps tell her the full story, Edward,' Francis suggested, to a withering glare from his professional companion.

'Yes, please do,' Elizabeth added coldly, 'although it has come to a sorry pass when you have to be reminded of the need for a husband to be truthful to his wife in all matters.'

Edward sighed. 'Very well, but I have not lied to you regarding the reason why we journey to Quorndon. I have merely withheld the extent of the danger of the mission. We do indeed ride under assumed identities in order to discover for ourselves what this man Marlowe and his companions are about. Burghley has reason to believe that they are planning to place on the throne another who is of royal blood, but more sympathetic to the Catholic cause.'

'And who is this person?' Elizabeth demanded.

Edward shook his head. 'It is as well that I do not disclose her identity.'

'*Her?*' Elizabeth echoed. 'A woman? Surely, when the Scots Mary was executed…'

Edward raised his hand urgently in a gesture for silence. 'Speak more softly, my sweet, and of other matters. Her identity is of no concern to any of us, beyond the fact that she exists, and that Marlowe and his band are suspected of plotting for her to replace Elizabeth on the throne. We may be overheard by the wrong people.'

'There is danger, even here?' Elizabeth turned to look all around her. 'Danger from what?'

'From *whom*,' Francis corrected her, then looked sternly at Edward. 'I would not have exposed my wife to any of this, had I a wife. But Elizabeth must be advised of the full extent of it, Edward, if only so that she is prepared to proceed circumspectly in all that follows.'

Edward took Elizabeth's hand, kissed it, and looked firmly into her eyes. 'These men we shall encounter in Quorndon are those we suspect of having killed the two royal justices, a town prostitute called Mary Chalmers, and a prisoner awaiting trial called Robert Cropper — all with a view to covering their tracks regarding their true purpose. That true purpose is an armed uprising against Her Majesty.'

Elizabeth went pale and rose from her bench. 'That completes my resolve — I shall ride back alone!'

'Along dangerous tracks, even in daylight?' Edward protested. 'I cannot let you take that risk.'

'Then come back with me,' said Elizabeth. 'Or do you have no concern for the safety of the woman you married, since you thought to drag her into a den of murderers? Why should you risk *my* life as well as your own for a queen who sits safely in London, requiring others to hazard their lives in order to keep her in her rich lifestyle? For shame, Edward! You owe her nothing, and me everything — where do your true loyalties lie?'

'Do you recall your final days at Wollaton Hall?' Edward asked. 'The life you led then, serving the daughter of the Willoughby family whose head forbade us to meet, let alone to make plans for our wedding? Who was it who made it possible for us to marry?'

Elizabeth hesitated for a moment, then nodded her concession. 'It is true that without Her Majesty's intervention, I would not now be Mistress Mountsorrel — or is it Mistress Marshall?'

'That will depend upon the decision you make in the next few minutes,' Edward said, grim-faced. 'I did not reveal the full extent of the danger we shall all be in because I did not wish to make you afraid.'

'Are you not afraid?' she challenged him. 'You will bare your throat to be slit by a gang of ruthless murderers, simply because you wish to preserve the life of privilege led by Her Majesty?'

'Such is my sworn duty as a guardian of the Queen's Peace,' Edward reminded her. 'You were fully aware of my office before we were married. As for fear, I experience it every day of my working life. I am called upon to protect my fellow men, women and children in the queen's name against all manner of evil, and not a day passes when I am not conscious of the risk I take in fulfilling my vow. But I fear something else more strongly, and that is the loss of you. If you are determined to return to town, then I shall of course accompany you to ensure your safety. But be advised that once you have been safely returned, I will have to return along this road to Quorndon, in order to discharge the duty imposed upon me.'

Elizabeth's face had softened during this short speech, and a tear appeared at the corner of each eye. She pulled Edward to his feet and embraced him. 'You were not meant to know, but every day when you leave to carry out your duties I say a prayer to God to keep you safe. That's why I dislike it so much when you rise while I'm still asleep, and slip from the house before I can kiss you farewell. I never know if I will see your lovely face reappear on the doorstep at the end of the day. I couldn't imagine life without you, and I couldn't bear to leave you to go down to Quorndon on your own. I would live each day in a torment of worry, not knowing if you were still alive. So I shall continue with you, foolhardy though your mission may seem. At least we might die together, which I would prefer to the prospect of living on without you.'

'Now you know why I never married,' Francis said as he wiped tears from his face.

'I'm sorry we've taken so long to visit, but please make my husband welcome,' Elizabeth said to the elderly couple who sat in adjacent chairs, taking in the last of the afternoon sun outside their grace-and-favour cottage next to the lodge gates of the Zouche estate.

The elderly woman rose eagerly but unsteadily to her feet and threw her arms around Elizabeth with a cry of delight, while the man looked on with a broad smile and rheumy eyes that welled with tears. Edward moved forward and held out his hand for the old man to shake.

'I believe you are Edward,' the old man said. 'My name is Edwin Porter. I trust that you will forgive me if I do not rise from my chair, but my back does not allow me to do so with any degree of comfort these days.'

'Of course,' Edward said, 'and neither of you must think any less of your beautiful and gracious daughter for the fact that this meeting is so long delayed. My duties have not permitted it until now.'

'You uphold the law in the adjoining county, do you not?' Edwin asked.

Edward nodded. 'Indeed I do, and in these troubled times it is a duty that allows me little spare time.'

'But time enough to give us grandchildren, I hope?' Elizabeth's mother, Catherine, enquired. She stepped back to look at Elizabeth's stomach in her dark brown travelling gown.

Elizabeth gave a light laugh that was almost a tinkle as she dismissed the enquiry. 'All in good time,' she assured her mother. 'But how do you both fare in your retirement years?'

'Your father pleads boredom,' Catherine explained, 'but whether it is with my company or the lack of daily routine, I have yet to determine. For myself nothing much has changed, since I am still required to cook and clean, as I always did even when we had our own apartments in the big house. On the subject of which, you must have smelt the apples cooking, and there will be enough pie left over for supper, always assuming that you will grace us with one night under our roof.'

'We'd like nothing more than to spend the night under your roof, Mama,' Elizabeth assured her before Edward could think of any alternative. 'We must, however, leave immediately after breakfast on the morrow, since we journey to Quorndon.'

Three hours later, they were finishing off the apple pie and enjoying a glass of elderflower brandy from Edwin's homemade supply.

'What business takes you to Quorndon?' he asked Edward.

Edward shot Elizabeth a warning glance as he replied, 'I'm afraid I'm not at liberty to divulge the details, but it's a routine matter that I've been asked to investigate on behalf of my employer. Do you know aught of the family who own the Nether Hall estate?'

'Only their names,' Edwin replied. 'The Farnhams were occasional visitors here at the Zouche house in the days when I was its steward, and before the Hastings family who own this estate transferred their interests to Codnor following their marriage into the Gainsford family. The castle you see further up the drive is neglected at present, and the household is much diminished from those days in which there were more than seventy servants, over whom my wife and I presided in our respective offices.'

'I well remember those days,' Elizabeth recalled with a dreamy smile. 'There was always much coming and going, and rumours abounded throughout the kitchen and outbuildings that we had a royal princess hidden away somewhere.'

'So we did,' Catherine confirmed. 'It was I who was responsible for ensuring that she had a modicum of comfort in her chamber, although she was not here for long before she was transferred elsewhere and eventually executed.'

'You speak of the Scots Mary?' Edward asked eagerly.

Edwin nodded. 'In those days, of course, we were forbidden to speak of her. But it is said that the master's loyalty to Her Majesty Queen Elizabeth saw him raised to high office as head of the Council of the North. Now he spends most of his time in York, while the castle here at Ashby falls sadly into disrepair.'

'What of the Farnhams?' Edward persisted. 'Did they ally with your master in his support for Elizabeth?'

'Of that I have no idea,' Edwin replied. 'It was said that relations between the Hastings and Farnham families cooled somewhat around the time of the Armada, although the reason for that was never revealed. There has certainly been no contact in recent years of which I am aware. Here, let me refill your mug.'

Later that night, Edward and Elizabeth lay down on the bedding prepared for them in the small back room of the cottage that doubled as a scullery.

'Why did you persist in questioning my father about the family residing at Nether Hall?' Elizabeth asked.

'I hope I did not do so either obviously or rudely,' Edward replied, 'but the more I can learn regarding the loyalties of the Farnhams, the easier our mission will be. If they are indeed harbouring traitors, then one would expect them to have a history of dissemblance. I found it significant that relations between the Farnhams and the fiercely loyal Hastings family who created this estate seem to have soured when they played their part in suppressing the Catholic threat posed by the Scots Mary.'

'You suspect the Farnhams — is that why we are headed to Nether Hall?'

'It is not I who suspects them, but Burghley. And yes, that's why we must lose no time in making our way south tomorrow, although it's tempting to remain here, away from the unpleasantness of the life I've chosen.'

'And which I've chosen to share with you,' Elizabeth reminded him as she snuggled closer. 'My mother thinks that you are very handsome and gallant, by the way.'

'And what does her daughter think?' Edward asked.

'I believe that I've already answered that question, so do not fish for compliments. I also got the feeling that my father respects you. I think he always felt reluctant to allow me to be exposed to the false flattery of some of the fops who would visit the master here, when I was a lady's maid. But my mother felt that it was the only way I might make a suitable match. How wrong she was, I'm delighted to say. Now, hold me tight while we get some sleep ahead of this latest venture of yours. Sorry, I meant of course this venture of *ours*.'

The next day, as they rode south under the warm morning sun, she had more questions for Edward.

'If we must play the parts of Master and Mistress Marshall, we must agree on what to say regarding your previous life.'

'That's easy,' said Edward. 'We tell the truth regarding my life up to the point at which I became a bailiff. I was an abandoned orphan, handed by a kindly clergyman to a poorhouse orphanage, from which I sneaked out one dark moonless night and found work on the Grey estate at Groby. While there I joined the Leicestershire Trained Band, which was taken south to join the troops under Robert Dudley, Earl of Leicester. We gathered at Tilbury to hear Elizabeth's inspiring address as we stood to defy the Spaniards who were believed to be heading up the Thames. But after the defeat of the Armada, all the troops were discharged without either bonus or the means of survival, and I have been wandering, disillusioned, ever since. I now wish to try my hand at being a strolling player. The story makes me perfect for possible recruitment into Marlowe's treasonous assembly.'

'I hope I shall be able to remember all that,' Elizabeth replied anxiously.

Edward chuckled. 'There may be no need. Not every wife is apprised of every detail of her husband's former life, and if there are apparent gaps in the story, this may serve to make me seem even more mysterious. Now, let us urge our horses to a swifter pace, since Francis will already be installed somewhere in Quorndon.'

10

The fields to their left led towards a slowly running river as they trotted their mounts into Quorndon. There was a central green, around which several humble cottages were grouped. In the middle of these was what appeared to be an inn. It was well past midday, and Edward and Elizabeth were tired and dust-covered, so they needed little additional reason to hitch their horses to a convenient pole outside the inn and make their way inside.

As their eyes adjusted to the gloom, a familiar voice hailed them from behind the counter.

Edward grinned as he walked over. 'Two pots of your best, please, good fellow. And perhaps some bread and cheese, if you have such available.'

Behind the counter, dressed from neck to knees in a white smock, Francis smiled back. 'By the looks of you, you have travelled far, and must be in need of refreshment and a good rest. If you would care to walk through to the garden at the rear, you will find an arbour. The shade will protect you from the afternoon sun, and you may sit to rest your aching limbs. I will bring your ale and victuals through to you as you take your ease.'

'You finally found your true vocation,' Edward teased as Francis joined them in the yard to the rear of the inn, carrying a tray on which their pots of ale and platters of bread and cheese were carefully balanced.

Francis chuckled as he put the tray on the table, looked quickly behind him and lowered his voice. 'All those years of intervening in alehouse brawls while working as a constable certainly proved advantageous,' he confided. 'I was only here for one night — last night, as it transpires — and was seated quietly in the main room there, minding my own business, when the perfect opportunity arose. A loud-mouthed oaf who it seems often causes trouble in here — and who apparently belongs with that crowd of malcontents skulking in Nether Hall — took offence at something said by the landlord when he spat into the sawdust. The next thing I knew, the landlord had been hauled over his counter, there was ale everywhere, and the young woman who works here was screaming like a stuck pig. Without thinking, I got up and solved the problem by sending the ill-mannered donkey back out through the front door on his arse. When he sought to come back in, wielding a sword, I demonstrated my disapproval by disabling his arm and confiscating his weapon. He was back this morning with a suitable apology, a monetary gift in exchange for the return of his sword, and a solemn promise never to behave in that fashion again.'

'And in consequence you were invited to remain here in order to discourage any similar behaviour in the future?' Edward asked with a broad smile.

'It relieved me of any need to invent a false reason for my presence here until such time as you need me to ride hard back into town,' Francis explained. 'I am promised three meals a day, a few coins at the end of the week, and a roof above my head. And by the looks I've been receiving from Nell, the landlord's niece who serves the pots, I shall not lack a warm companion on chilly evenings. So all in all it is looking favourable. But how fare you? Have you yet approached our mark in Nether Hall?'

'No, we have only just arrived in Quorndon,' Edward advised him. 'We were persuaded to remain overnight in Ashby.'

'Well, you will find the Hall down the road half a league towards Mountsorrel,' said Francis. 'Just after you cross a stream there is a track to the left that leads across a meadow. The River Soar is then crossed by a footbridge, and from the centre rise of that you can see the roof of the Hall. Or so Nell told me when I asked her.'

'And what reason did you give her for that enquiry?' Edward asked nervously.

'I told her that I was a wealthy soldier of fortune in search of employment as a footman or suchlike, whereupon she made me a certain promise that inclines me to remain here instead, in order to have it fulfilled. And so I combine business with pleasure. Now, if you will excuse me, I believe I have other customers seeking my services back there.'

He pocketed the coins that Edward had given him in payment for their repast, then strolled purposefully back inside with the empty tray.

Elizabeth looked anxiously into Edward's eyes. 'Surely, what Francis had to impart was good news — why did your face become so gloomy?'

'It was the reference to Mountsorrel,' he replied with a shudder. 'It reminded me that this is the district of my birth, and that somewhere around here I was conceived, then just as easily abandoned.'

'Well, *this* woman has no intention of abandoning you,' Elizabeth reassured him as she kissed his cheek. 'So let us refresh ourselves before we test our false identities down the road.'

Given the fact that it was almost the height of midsummer, there was still plenty of late evening sunlight to guide Edward and Elizabeth over the river bridge. A few minutes later, they trotted into the yard of a generously proportioned country mansion with three jettied storeys. There was a set of stables to one side, and they had just dismounted and handed their bridles to a young boy when they were challenged by a loud voice.

'Who are you, and what is your business here?'

Edward and Elizabeth turned in unison, and found themselves addressed by a red-bearded giant of a man who was dressed like a fine courtier. He brandished a sword in his left hand, while his right was strapped to his chest with a bandage. Hoping that this was not the man he had come to meet, since the odds were that he was the same individual who had recently come second in a contest with Francis, Edward opted for a haughty tone.

'My business is none of yours, unless you be Master Marlowe, who I am here to meet. As for my identity, that will be revealed only to him.'

The man gave a sickly sneer. 'It is my business to ensure that none pass through to the house unless they give good account of themselves. So, I ask again, what is your business?'

'And once again I advise you that my business is none of yours!' Edward shouted back. 'So I would be obliged if you would advise Master Marlowe that Edward Marshall wishes to have an audience with him.'

'I am no man's page!' the man replied angrily, waving his sword in the air.

Elizabeth grabbed Edward's arm as she whispered, 'Have a care, Edward — the man clearly means to set about you if you do not reveal your reason for being here.'

'With only one arm?' Edward replied dismissively. He allowed himself an arrogant smirk and spoke loudly enough to be heard by his challenger. 'By the looks of this poltroon, he has recently come off worse against an opponent. I'll warrant that the arm with which he would be obliged to wield that sword is not the one he would employ for preference. So either advise your master that Edward Marshall wishes to see him, or I will go through you and advise him myself.'

'Edward Marshall clearly has a high opinion of himself,' came a reedy voice from the open doorway of the house beyond the courtyard. A man stepped out from under its shadow. 'And either he is very brave and experienced in swordplay, or he is a rank fool. Either way, he has a commanding voice that I could employ to good effect. Stand back, Eustace, and let me converse with him.'

The man stepped back with a snarl, turned on his heel and stormed towards the house. As he passed the man in the doorway, he muttered, 'There is an old adage about having a dog and barking oneself. If he sets about you, look to your own safety and do not blame me.'

'You must forgive my companion,' said the new arrival as he moved towards Edward. 'What he possesses in bravery he lacks in gallantry and fine manners. I am Christopher Marlowe, and you may now state both your name and your business.'

Edward made a quick assessment of the man he had come to spy on, the man who allegedly commanded an armed host capable of murderous deeds, and tried not to laugh out loud. He was the very opposite of a military commander, with a slender frame of average height and a boyish face surrounded by flowing locks. His beard and moustache were either severely trimmed or reluctant to grow any longer.

'My name is Edward Marshall,' Edward began. 'I am a former soldier of fortune now fallen upon hard times who seeks to explore the opportunities that are said to be open in the world of masques and mummeries. In short, I would trade my sword for a parchment of fine words that I might proclaim out loud in return for rich reward in royal palaces and the houses of the wealthy.'

'And the woman?' Marlowe enquired, almost as if Elizabeth were Edward's horse. 'She washes your raiment, or acts as your muse, perhaps?'

'She is my wife,' Edward retorted hotly, 'and while I would not wish to pick an argument with you at this early stage in our acquaintance, I must counsel you to speak more respectfully of her.'

'And if I do not choose to do so?' Marlowe taunted him.

Edward ensured that he was standing at his full height. 'Then I shall, should I prove merciful, simply turn on my heel and depart in search of some other wordsmith, although I am advised that there are none better than yourself. In a less merciful humour, I would spread your innards across your doorstep.'

He felt Elizabeth stiffen in horror at the risk he was taking, but Marlowe merely laughed, as if observing the antics of a juggler at a summer fair.

'You clearly present as a man with spirit. If it is not simply the guile of a talented player, pray advise me — whence came your courage?'

'From my heart, wherein may be found every man's courage,' Edward replied in an effort to sound like a man gifted with a poetic turn of phrase. 'But if the true import of your enquiry is where I acquired my martial confidence, then be advised that I stood with the Earl of Leicester among the trained bands that were assembled at Tilbury to resist the Spanish foe. Such was our reputation for valour that the Spaniards took themselves elsewhere, and I was left to fend for myself, living by my wits.'

'You were not selected by Leicester himself to join his inner core of bodyguards?' Marlowe enquired.

This question revealed to Edward that Marlowe was not simply a mindless fop. Robert Dudley had indeed hand-picked a retinue of his own from the three thousand or so at Tilbury, and while Edward had not been among them he had been sent away with a letter of recommendation to the sheriffs of both Nottinghamshire and Leicestershire. Thanking his stars that he had not chosen the county in which they were now standing, Edward made intelligent use of what knowledge he had of subsequent events.

'I was selected to train those to whom you refer, but fate took my patron from me. Leicester died just weeks after commissioning me, and Her Majesty has proved less than gracious to those who were prepared to lay down their lives in her service. I have wandered from estate to estate, sometimes as a footman and bodyguard, and at other times as a hewer of wood and tender of horses. While I was working at the Lacey house in Cotgrave, I learned of a body of fine players who had but recently left, and who were led by a man whose fine prose seems destined to set the mark for all others of his calling. I would now try my hand at something that appeals to me more than hacking limbs from either trees or adversaries in battle.'

'You have retained your soldierly skills?' Marlowe enquired.

Edward shrugged. 'In truth I have not, of late, had occasion to test them, which is perhaps a matter to be celebrated by the oaf you called "Eustace" just now. One step more and he would have been without his *other* arm.'

Marlowe laughed, although his eyes narrowed as he pursued a subtle line of enquiry. 'You thought highly of the late Robert Dudley?'

'As a commander of men, certainly. As my patron, without a doubt. As a man — well, that was another matter entirely. To speak plainly, he was a braggart who hid behind the queen's skirts and relied upon her favouritism to avoid facing any consequences for his womanising, his idle boasting and his all-consuming ambition. He also made much of a purported adherence to the Protestant cause in order to retain Her Majesty's protection, when to my mind he was an atheist of the worst degree — a man who turned his back on the true faith to feign adherence to a blasphemous regime in which he had no true belief.'

'You speak like a man who might well have fled the realm when Elizabeth became queen,' Marlowe replied suspiciously. 'You are aware that to refer to the Church of Rome as "the true faith" invites incarceration within the Tower?'

'I do not do so openly,' Edward replied with a confident smile, 'since I am clearly aware of the fate that has befallen others who have done so. What I believe in private is another matter, and — if I might make so bold — none of your business.'

'But you would fight for what you believe in?' Marlowe persevered.

Edward nodded. 'Perhaps more appropriately, I would fight for *who* I believe in, although that is not the reason for my presence here today. I wish to join a company of players, not a private army. I have seen too much warfare, and not enough true art.'

Marlowe glanced up at the sky. 'I sense that the evening chill is not long away, and you and your lady must be both weary and hungry after your journey from Cotgrave. Come in, and we shall see whether or not that fine voice and warrior bearing of yours might be put to better use than wandering the highways.'

He led them through the entrance and down a wood-panelled hallway that opened out into a sizeable main hall with a long table down its centre. There were portraits on the walls and an upper gallery for musicians. A serving boy appeared from a doorway towards the far end, and Marlowe raised his voice.

'Ask Mistress Strong to have wine, bread and meats brought in for our recent arrivals.' He turned back to Edward with a smile, then walked across to a desk at the side of the chamber, from which he removed several sheets of vellum. Then he invited Edward and Elizabeth to take a seat on the bench to one side of the centre table, and handed the sheets to Edward.

'This is a tragedy that I recently penned, and it is one of those that has been played to great acclaim in several wealthy houses of late. It is entitled *Tamburlaine the Great*, and it tells of the rise of a humble shepherd to become the conqueror of all that he sets his sights upon. He is a ruthless warrior driven by his own self-belief to acts of inhuman cruelty — in short, a Colossus not to be trifled with. Pray indulge me for a moment by reading these two lines above my finger here.'

Edward looked at the lines, took a deep breath and boomed, 'I hold the Fates bound fast in iron chains, and with my hand turn Fortune's wheel about!'

'Excellent!' Marlowe enthused. 'You have exactly the appropriate degree of raw power and fatal arrogance. Now, the ultimate test. Please walk to the far end of this chamber with this page, read what is written thereon, and proclaim it to me in your most commanding voice.'

Edward moved across the room, looked briefly down at the parchment, absorbed its general flavour and bellowed:

'The world will strive with hosts of men-at-arms

To swarm unto the ensign I support.

The host of Xerxes, which by fame is said

To drink the mighty Parthian Araris,

Was but a handful to that we will have:

Our quivering lances, shaking in the air,

And bullets, like Jove's dreadful thunderbolts,

Enroll'd in flames and fiery smouldering mists,

Shall threat the gods more than Cyclopian wars.

And with our sun-bright armour, as we march,

We'll chase the stars from heaven, and dim their eyes

That stand and muse at our admired arms.'

Edward felt self-conscious at having been overdramatic, and looked back at Marlowe with a flush of embarrassment on his cheeks. But Marlowe was on his feet, applauding and waving Edward back to his seat, while Elizabeth simply sat there with an open mouth.

'Splendid, dear man!' Marlowe enthused as Edward climbed back onto the bench, both surprised and delighted that he appeared to have passed as a proclaimer of verse. 'How quickly do you think you can memorise some fifty pages such as that? It is important that you do not simply read out the words. Instead, you must proclaim them as if they had just come into your mind, like a man in the grip of a powerful force.'

'You wish me to play the part?' Edward asked.

Marlowe nodded. 'As soon as you have familiarised yourself with it. We ride north in a week or so, and will be offering it in one of the most noble houses in Derbyshire.'

'But surely there is already someone in your company with the requisite skills?' Edward objected.

'Indeed there is, but he lacks your handsome features, and is somewhat hampered in his portrayal of an invincible warrior by the fact that one arm is currently held in a cradle of cloth. He is Eustace Dempsey, the man who challenged you on your approach here. The fool got himself into some contest with an oaf in a local alehouse who he has sworn to go back and kill. Should he do so, we shall of course be required to depart from here even earlier, but at present you have a week to prepare yourself for your first performance as a member of The Marlowe Company of Players. As if to convey the approval of the gods of such a fortuitous arrival as yours, here comes Mistress Strong with our supper.'

While Marlowe had been speaking, a tall, gaunt woman with short, greying hair had silently entered the hall. She resembled the abbess of a convent both in her face and choice of attire, and carried a platter of cold meats and bread. Behind her walked the serving boy from earlier, with a tray that contained a large jug and three goblets. As she laid her platter down on the board, she fixed her cold, grey eyes on Marlowe and announced, 'Your supper, Master Marlowe.'

'Excellent!' Marlowe exclaimed. 'And what exquisite timing.' He turned to Edward and Elizabeth and effected the introductions. 'This is the housekeeper here at Nether Hall, Mistress Strong. Mistress, please welcome the latest member of our company, Master Edward Marshall and his wife, whose name I do not yet know.'

Elizabeth quickly introduced herself. Mistress Strong gave the faintest of nods in acknowledgement and transferred her gaze to Edward. Then her eyes opened wide, she turned deathly pale, and her jaw dropped.

Edward's stomach churned as he realised that he'd been recognised.

11

'How could she possibly know you?' Elizabeth argued as she and Edward lay in their allotted chamber on the third floor of Nether Hall. 'She seems quite at home here, so it's unlikely that she's ever been to Nottingham. And you left this area as a baby when some clergyman or other consigned you to the Leicester orphanage, and you haven't been back since, so there can be no local connection. You must simply have been imagining things — after all, it *was* a nervous time for both of us. But thanks to your fine display we seem to have been accepted here, so just console yourself with that and get some sleep.'

'It was the way her jaw dropped when she laid eyes on me,' Edward explained. 'It wasn't one of those situations in which you see a face and spend a few moments remembering where you've seen it before. It was as if she recognised me on the instant, and yet I'm sure I've never laid eyes on her before. It made me very uncomfortable, and I can only hope that it doesn't lead to our true identities being discovered.'

'There's no reason to believe that it will,' Elizabeth reassured him as she drew him close. 'Now, let's do something to take our minds off the unnerving business of subterfuge.'

The following morning they ate a generous breakfast, supervised by Mistress Strong. Edward felt as if her sharp grey eyes pierced through his armour of pretence. After they had eaten, he and Elizabeth went outside and sat on a bench beside a herb garden. This gave access to a fallow field in which a group of men were engaging in physical exercise under the command of an older man, whose bearing was that of a seasoned military veteran.

Edward was engaged in an attempt to commit to memory the pages and pages of dense dialogue that seemed to involve only the part he was to play. He was not comfortable with such a task, since the written word had never been presented for his perusal in such a flowery and exaggerated form, and he had never before been required to commit so many lines to memory. He therefore groaned when he saw Marlowe strolling purposefully towards them.

'I take it that your chamber was comfortable?' he said breezily as he drew level with them, and they both assured him that it was. Then he nodded down at the pages of vellum in Edward's hand. 'How do you progress in learning your part?'

Edward frowned. 'The dialogue is very rich, and I doubt that I shall be able to commit so much of it to memory in such a short time. When do we head north, did you say?'

'Not for a week at least,' Marlowe assured him as he gazed out into the field where the men were exercising. 'The players need to shed some of their winter fat.'

'Why do you have them exercising like soldiers?' Edward asked. 'It reminds me of my days in the Trained Band, when we would walk up and down the country lanes for hours on end.'

'Do you perhaps wish to join the other men?' Marlowe enquired eagerly.

Edward responded with a vigorous shake of the head. 'I do not remember those days with fondness, and I do not believe that I have any need to lose weight.'

'Indeed you do not,' Marlowe agreed, 'since we must present you as a most imposing warrior, a gargantuan among men — a Colossus among mere mortals.'

'But a shepherd nevertheless?' Edward countered. 'My various employments around the nation have required that I associate with shepherds, and I never yet encountered one who could be described as you have written the part of Tamburlaine.'

'That is the entire thrust of the drama,' Marlowe explained. 'Tamburlaine knew of his destiny from his earliest days. It was as if the gods had whispered in his ear that he would grow from being a shepherd boy to a great commander of men. When you take his part, you must never act the humble shepherd — always the born leader. But I see that we are to be joined by our gracious and accommodating housekeeper.'

Mistress Strong had been making her way from the house with a basket of linen, heading for a line that had been slung between two trees. She smiled in their direction as Edward instinctively buried his head behind his manuscript, then she took a few moments to drape the wet bed linen across the rope before walking back to them with her empty basket.

'I always found washing to be the most exhausting of tasks,' said Elizabeth in an effort to divert the housekeeper's attention from Edward. 'Does the estate not have a washerwoman?'

'It does ordinarily,' Mistress Strong replied, 'but she dwells in the village, and is currently being called upon to minister to her elderly father, who is not long for this life. The laundry duties have therefore fallen back upon me.'

'Do you need any assistance?' Elizabeth asked eagerly. 'While I will own that washing is not my favourite household task, there are others in which I might be of use to you. I was brought up to domestic service when my mother occupied a similar role to yours on the Ashby estate. I also grow bored listening to my husband pretending that he is engaged in conquering the world.'

A suggestion of a smile crossed Mistress Strong's lips as she accepted Elizabeth's offer of assistance. As the two women made their way back to the house, Marlowe took Elizabeth's vacated seat and Edward turned to look at him with a concerned expression.

'You heard what she said? If even my own wife finds my performance less than absorbing, what hope might I have of entrancing strangers?'

Marlowe laughed in the way that Edward was already finding intensely irritating. 'Those houses of the wealthy in which we shall be presenting our tragedy have no real appreciation of the art of dramatic display. They seek only diversion from their humdrum existence, and they pay well, in addition to providing a generous board. Some of them even find that my offerings take them back to a former age whose passing they mourn.'

'The age of chivalry, you mean?' Edward enquired as he took in the new exercises that the men in the field were engaging in. 'The days of bold knights, lovelorn ladies, tournaments in the tiltyards and suchlike? Is that why your players are now being trained in the use of the crossbow — a weapon that was abandoned not long after we had lost any claim to lands in France?'

'I had all but forgotten that you have had recent experience of military warfare,' said Marlowe. 'The crossbows are for exercise only, since they require great physical strength to draw them back into a firing position.'

Edward looked at Marlowe with raised eyebrows. 'It is easy to see that you have no recent military experience of your own, Master Marlowe. While there was a time in which a man needed strength in either his forearms or his legs with which to cock a crossbow for firing, these days it may be achieved even by a woman, and certainly by a young boy, by the use of what they call a "crannequin", a ratcheted lever that winds back the bolt to its firing position. Even so, the crossbow has not been employed by English armies since long before the date of your birth, and certainly not in my time. And if, as you say, those players of yours are employing crossbows simply for the physical exercise involved, why do they appear to be firing them at targets hung from the trees?'

Marlowe looked uncomfortable for a moment, then appeared to regain his composure. 'For that, you must blame the man who is instructing them, and who cannot forget that once he commanded an entire wing of His Majesty's army.'

'*His* Majesty?' Edward enquired. 'Given that queens have sat upon the English throne for the past four decades, the man to whom you refer must be almost ancient. Yet you entrust him with the task of ensuring that your men remain fit? Fit for *what*, precisely?'

'He is our host, Master Marshall, and we must humour him if we are to remain here until we depart for Derbyshire. He is Sir Ralph Farnham, and he was present when the former King Henry laid siege to Boulogne.'

'And he teaches outmoded forms of warfare to men who are primarily recruited as strolling players?'

'Purely exercises that will ensure their fitness, as I already explained. They are required to take to the road between engagements on country estates.'

'And this next estate — the one on which I shall make my first entrance as Tamburlaine — it is in Derbyshire, you say?'

'Indeed it is, and perhaps the finest in that county. You have heard of Chatsworth, perhaps?'

'I have been there,' Edward said as his heart sank at the prospect of being recognised as they passed through Nottinghamshire on their way north. In truth he had never set foot on the Chatsworth estate, but he remembered what Burghley had told him about those who resided there.

'In what capacity?' Marlowe asked.

Edward shrugged deprecatingly. 'Purely as a day labourer, in return for food and shelter. I was there for the bringing in of their latest harvest, before returning south. As I recall, there is a young lady residing there who is of royal blood.'

'There is a very old lady living there who has just buried her fourth husband, and is one of the wealthiest women in the realm. She has estates all over the north of England through her marriage to the Earl of Shrewsbury.'

'You refer to Bess Cavendish, do you not?' Edward probed. 'She who has the wardship of a young lady named Arbella Stuart?'

'For a mere wandering discharged soldier, you appear to be possessed of a great deal of knowledge regarding the nobility,' Marlowe replied coldly as he rose to leave. 'And you ask too many questions. See to memorising your part.'

Elizabeth was more guarded in her conversation once she realised that Mistress Strong had agreed to allow her to assist in the work of the household only in order that she might pump her for information regarding her husband.

They were in the great hall, dusting the frames of the portraits that hung from the walls, which appeared to depict former members of the Farnham dynasty. Elizabeth was setting about the task with a dexterity that impressed Mistress Strong, and she paused her dusting to call across the hall.

'Would I be correct in my belief that you have done this before?' she enquired.

'On the Ashby estate, Mistress, I was taught all aspects of the work,' Elizabeth replied.

'Please call me Margaret, since we are clearly going to be working together. As for the Ashby estate, the Farnham family who own this estate were once regular visitors there. I recall accompanying Lady Ursula when she was still alive, and I was employed here at the time as her lady's maid.'

'I was just a girl in those days, of course,' said Elizabeth, 'but even I can recall the excitement when the Farnhams were due to pay us a visit. But then there seemed to be a cooling between the two families.'

'Indeed, religion has a lot to answer for,' Margaret nodded sadly. 'Which reminds me: these portraits have to be taken down, dusted on the other side, and re-hung in time for this evening's gathering.'

This was the first intimation Elizabeth had received that the portraits might be double-sided, and she stretched to lift down the heavy gilt frame of the one that she had been in the process of dusting. She turned it around, and on its reverse side was a depiction of a Christian saint being lifted into Heaven by a group of angels with outstretched arms. She glanced quickly at the painting that Margaret had reversed, and on its other side was the portrait of either a cardinal or a Pope. She was just making a mental note to pass on this significant piece of information to Edward when Margaret broke into her thoughts.

'I assume that you are not one of those who follows the Protestant way to the point of seeking to persecute those of the old faith?'

'In truth, Margaret,' said Elizabeth, 'religion has never played a great part in my life. I was obliged to attend the local parish church in Wollaton when I was lady's maid to the daughter of the Willoughby family, but I whiled away the seemingly empty two hours with thoughts of my own.'

Margaret nodded to one of the benches alongside the long centre table. 'Let us rest for a moment, and you can tell me how a lady's maid to a family as wealthy and exalted as the Willoughbys came to be the wife of a footloose soldier of fortune. You *are* married, I assume?'

'Of course we are,' Elizabeth confirmed as she took a seat.

'There are no children?' Margaret probed.

Elizabeth shook her head. 'Not as yet, but we have only been married for a matter of months.'

'So how did you meet?'

'Edward came to the estate looking for work,' Elizabeth lied in accordance with the false story she and Edward had agreed upon. 'He was given work with the deer in the park, and we began talking when all the staff were gathered for meals in the kitchen. He is, you must own, a most handsome man, and he swept me off my feet with his tales of his days serving under the Earl of Leicester, his sight of Queen Elizabeth, and his desire to be better than Dame Fortune has allowed him.'

'What of his early days, his parents, his home?' Margaret enquired. 'Did he disclose aught of that to you, or have you committed yourself in marriage to a former soldier of fortune who, for all you know, may have come from bad seed?'

'As for that,' Elizabeth replied, 'it transpires that he is an orphan. He tells me that he was left in a church doorway by his birth mother, and taken in by a kindly priest to an orphanage not far from here, in Leicester somewhere, from which he escaped and found estate work on a large property. From there he opted to join a local militia band and was taken down to London by the Earl of Leicester, where he had the privilege of being addressed by Her Majesty. But once the Spanish threat had been overcome, he, like many others, was cast adrift to fend for himself. He clearly has more about him than should be wasted in field labour, so perhaps if he makes a success of this latest venture with Master Marlowe we may look forward to better days.'

'He is still young enough, I would imagine,' Margaret observed. 'I would estimate that he has not yet seen twenty-five.'

'He has no information regarding his actual date of birth, obviously,' Elizabeth replied, 'but from what he was told he was born in March of 1563, which means that his next birthday will be his twenty-eighth. What is this "gathering" to which you made reference earlier, might I ask? Is it a rehearsal of the masque in which Edward is taking the leading role? I will need to wash and change my gown if that is the case.'

'There will be no need for that,' Margaret replied quite sharply. 'We women are not allowed to attend these gatherings, which occur several times a week. Should your husband be required, I feel sure that Master Marlowe will so advise him. Now, shall we continue to ensure that the hall is sufficiently prepared?'

Before supper, Elizabeth and Edward met up in their chamber.

'Has Marlowe said anything to you regarding a gathering of some sort in the great hall this evening?' Elizabeth asked him.

Edward shook his head, but was curious. 'What nature of gathering?'

'I know not. It was something that Margaret Strong told me when we were dusting the portraits that hang in the hall. They have religious themes on their reverse sides, by the way, so each of them must be set with two canvases, one on each side of the frame.'

'And this "gathering" is to take place in the hall?' Edward enquired, and Elizabeth nodded. 'From what Margaret said I believe that the art works will be reversed, so that instead of those tedious portraits of pompous old men there will be depictions of saints ascending to Heaven, cardinals, Popes and so on. It must surely be a Catholic Mass that they are planning, must it not?'

'So it would seem,' Edward nodded. 'If so, then this will confirm that whoever these people are, they are no friend to the ordained religion of this nation, and therefore probably no supporter of the queen who keeps their Roman religion suppressed. We may not be here as long as I had expected.'

'Should you request Marlowe's permission to attend?' Elizabeth asked.

Edward shook his head vigorously. 'I have, I fear, already alerted his suspicions regarding our true reason for being here, so I must devise some means of attending it without anyone's knowledge.'

'Should they require refreshment, I can perhaps contrive to be the one who serves it,' Elizabeth volunteered. 'I believe I have sufficiently gained the confidence of Mistress Strong that I can be entrusted with such a task. She has bid me call her "Margaret", and she seemed very interested in how we came to be together. I believe that she may have taken a shine to me, and intends to take me under her wing.'

'She may simply be seeking to report back to Marlowe regarding the real reason why we are here, so have a care,' Edward warned her. 'How much did you disclose?'

'Nothing more than we had agreed. I said you were an orphan who escaped from the poorhouse in Leicester and ventured south as a soldier, then took to wandering the highways and byways when your fortunes took a turn for the worse. That is all.'

'That is probably sufficient. Remember, if pressed, that I am very secretive by nature, and that there are aspects of my life that you suspect I am keeping hidden from you. Now, how might I seek to gain access to this gathering without being seen?'

'There appear to be galleries high up the wall of the hall in two of its corners,' Elizabeth reminded him. 'If they are the same that we had at Wollaton, then they are for musicians when they play at feasts and other celebrations.'

'How are they accessed?' Edward asked eagerly.

Elizabeth shook her head. 'I was never a musician, obviously, but I seem to recall having seen men entering the galleries in Wollaton Hall by way of a staircase hidden behind an arras.'

'Perfect!' Edward muttered. 'If I can gain access to one of those galleries, I may look down on the assembly and confirm what they are about. I may not even need to look down, if they are obliging enough to conduct their sacrilegious rites loudly enough. Perhaps I shall be able to excuse myself at supper and make my way behind the arras when everyone else is at board.'

Elizabeth frowned. 'There is to be no communal supper this evening, it seems. Margaret told me that our supper will be served here in our chamber, so I assume that it must be the same for everyone here.'

'Or they simply require that I be out of the way while they conduct their gathering, which is almost certainly a Mass,' Edward mused. 'We shall wait until our supper has been served, so that my absence from this chamber will not be noticed. While the others are still at their suppers, I shall creep down to the chamber behind the great hall and seek out this curtain that hides the minstrels' staircase.'

Two hours later, he slipped silently into the rear chamber by way of the service corridor that led from the kitchens, dressed in the grubby clothing in which he had first arrived, hoping to pass as a server. He could hear the excited hum from the great hall through the adjoining door as he smiled with satisfaction at the floor-length tapestry of a forest scene that hung, for no apparent reason, close to that adjoining door. Elizabeth's advice proved accurate, and he tiptoed up the creaking stairs, hoping that the chatter of male voices was masking the sound from his soft shoes on old wood.

He reached the top and lowered himself into a crouching position as he shuffled up to the gallery's guard rail, then allowed himself a glimpse over the edge. There were a dozen or more men kneeling in apparent supplication before an altar, which was richly decorated with gold cloth. A tall man in ecclesiastical robes had been reading out loud from some Latin text whose phrases were still audible as Edward knelt there and grinned triumphantly.

If this was not a Catholic Mass, then he was a carthorse. He had achieved the first half of the task allotted to him, and could now report back to Burghley that these men being housed in Nether Hall were covert followers of the proscribed religion. He now just needed to confirm that they were the ones responsible for four murders, and were plotting to usurp Elizabeth's throne. This might, he reminded himself, take a little longer.

12

'Do we have enough evidence against them to be able to instruct Francis to ride home and bring back the castle garrison?' Elizabeth asked eagerly when Edward had slipped back into their chamber and told her what he had observed.

He shook his head with a frown. 'While it is undoubtedly regarded as treasonous to observe secret Romanist rites, and while the Farnham estate is almost certainly concealing priests smuggled over from France, we are not here for that purpose, remember? We seek evidence that these are the people responsible for the recent murders in Nottingham and Costock; until we have that, we must leave Francis to enjoy his time carousing in the local inn.'

'How will you set about getting that evidence?'

Edward shrugged. 'Perhaps by showing a greater inclination to become involved in whatever they engage in when they venture into the field beyond the herb garden. In the meantime, I seem condemned to memorising that dreadfully complex prose written by Marlowe. Perhaps that is his only offence, since he doesn't seem to be inclined towards anything of a martial nature. I begin to suspect that the real leader of the men is that old duffer Farnham, and Marlowe is simply acting as some sort of diversionary. But until we know for certain, Francis must remain where he is.'

Three days later Edward was handed his opportunity. He was seated in his usual place on the bench by the herb garden, looking at the men assembling in the field below and seeking some diversion from the tedium of learning his lines when he heard a commanding voice behind him, calling his name. He turned to identify the speaker.

'It's Master Marshall, is it not?' Sir Ralph Farnham boomed. He was dressed as befitted a soldier in the ranks of those dragged across to France by the bellicose Henry VIII in his younger years. Presumably these were the very clothes that he had worn then, since the doublet under the cuirass was ripped and stained, and its leather straps were cracked. The man himself had clearly retired to a lifetime of eating and drinking, and it was doubtful whether these days his heart could withstand anything more strenuous than a walk from the kitchen to the dining room. Edward smiled up at the man and tried not to smirk.

'I am indeed he, and I am advised that you are our gracious host.'

'That is indeed my proud privilege. I am also training those men to battle readiness.'

'I was not aware that we are currently at war,' Edward replied.

Farnham frowned. 'Indeed not yet, but when Her Majesty dies, may we not expect an invasion from Scotland by the pretender James?'

'I wouldn't know,' Edward said as he feigned boredom and looked down at the papers in his hand. 'It is seemingly my destiny to merely *act* the part of a great warrior.'

'Believe me, it will happen,' Farnham assured him. 'James skulks across the border, awaiting his chance to avenge the death of his mother, the Scots traitor Mary. It is far better that Elizabeth be followed to the throne by someone more worthy of the name of "Tudor", rather than "Stuart".'

'And you know of such a person?' Edward enquired as casually as he could.

Farnham nodded, although the expression on his face was that of someone who sensed that he might have spoken too openly. 'I do indeed, but for the moment we must prepare an army to repel any incursion from Scotland. You once fought against the Spanish invasion, or so I am advised.'

'I was not called upon to do any fighting,' Edward cautioned, though he was anxious to have a justification for moving down into the training field.

'But you stood with Leicester at Tilbury, did you not, in defence of Elizabeth, just as I was in the ranks of warriors led by her father as we laid siege to Boulogne?'

'I *stood* with Leicester, certainly, but that was all we did. The Spanish were driven off by our navy, so there was no occasion to employ the skills in which we had been trained.'

'Do you still recall those skills, and would you be prepared to pass them on to the men you see in the field down there?' Farnham asked as Edward felt a shiver of anticipation. 'I grow too weak in the arm and lacking in wind to demonstrate the thrust, parry and cut that you were no doubt instructed in, and I would be in your debt should you agree to demonstrate them to the men. Apart from Eustace Dempsey there are none down there who have seen battle.'

'I am required to learn this lengthy part ahead of our performance in Chatsworth,' Edward offered as a half-hearted excuse that he hoped would be waved away.

'That tedious Marlowe is here at my sufferance, and will do as he is commanded,' said Farnham with a sneer. 'As for Chatsworth, we shall not venture north until the men are ready to join others who will await us there. It is important that when they do, they put up a braver show of organised military discipline. At present, they are fit for little more than isolated acts as cut-throats and highway robbers. Go down there and help me turn them into a fighting force to be reckoned with.'

A few minutes later, Elizabeth turned from her mirror in surprise as Edward reappeared in their chamber, in search of his sword.

'It is in that corner by the window,' she advised him. 'But why the haste?'

Instead of answering her question, he asked one of his own. 'What are you planning to do today?'

'Margaret Strong has asked me to assist with the preparation of today's dinner, since the cook has had a fever these past few days. Why do you ask?'

'Be ready to ride to the inn in the village and dispatch Francis north. I have been invited to join that band of cut-throats in military training, and I hope to learn all that I need to when I do so.'

'Will that not expose you to danger?'

'Of course it will, but how else to discharge the mission we have been set? Wish me luck.'

'You are going nowhere until you kiss me,' Elizabeth pouted. 'Or am I no longer attractive to you, now that I seem to have become a housemaid?'

'Of course you are, and my heartfelt apologies,' Edward said as he kissed her on the lips. 'Now, pray for my safe delivery from what I must do next.'

Back down in the exercise field, the men were ordered back to their feet by Farnham as he saw Edward striding purposefully towards them. He stooped, picked up two long tree branches that had been stripped down to form poles of approximately sword length, grunted from the effort of bending, then threw one to Edward.

'Master Marshall here was once a member of the army of the Earl of Leicester, and like myself was trained in the proper use of a sword,' Farnham announced. 'He will demonstrate better than I how it is done. Master Marshall, if you would be so obliging?'

For the next twenty minutes or so Edward used the tree branch to demonstrate the necessary body postures for "thrust", "cut" and "parry", while the men did their best to imitate his actions with sticks, broom handles and fence staves. Their actions — with the exception of Eustace Dempsey — were so clumsy and amateur that Edward was beginning to doubt whether these were the same men who'd ambushed the coach guarded by Tower soldiers and killed them all, along with the justice they'd been escorting. But then the atmosphere changed.

One of the men threw down his fence stave with a curse and yelled back at Edward, 'Why do we need these lessons in waving sticks about? We can kill just as easily with crossbows, and not half the effort is required.'

'There will be no crossbow practice today!' Farnham yelled from a few feet behind Edward. 'Instead you are being taught the far more important skill of hand-to-hand combat using swords.'

'Crossbows are for cowards anyway,' Edward observed, hoping to provoke a response, and he was not disappointed.

'Who are you to call us cowards?' Dempsey demanded, red-faced. 'You may once have sat on your arse while the Spaniards were blown off course by an ill wind, but you never saw combat, hand to hand, with an enemy soldier, and all you're fit for now is mincing around pretending to be a mighty warrior in some fancy masque written by that fool Marlowe. I can tell you, little man, that crossbows can be deadly when fired properly by men who have been trained in their use.'

'You have experience in that?' Edward demanded as he adopted a disdainful tone that was not entirely false.

Dempsey nodded vigorously and shouted, 'Indeed I have!'

'Not recently, I assume,' Edward replied as his pulse rate increased, 'since there have been no wars for many years, and to kill a man in times of peace is a crime.'

'Recently enough to know that crossbows can be deadly.'

'And, of course, they can be operated with only one arm,' Edward shot back with a meaningful stare at the sling on Dempsey's injured arm. 'Indeed it would be a suitable choice of weapon for a fool seeking to shoot a man in the back.'

'Damn you!' Dempsey bellowed as he pulled the sling from his arm, bent down, and picked up the sword he had discarded. 'Look to your guard, Master Braggart, and let's see who's the coward!'

'Enough!' Farnham yelled, but Edward was now sufficiently incensed to be beyond taking orders.

'Do not fear for my safety,' he called back over his shoulder, 'but I apprehend that you may shortly be called upon to give weapon training to a man with *no* arms.'

Dempsey gave a howl of outrage and charged towards Edward with his sword raised. Edward stepped backwards, throwing Dempsey off balance, reached out for his sword arm, and twisted. Although it was not his injured arm, Dempsey gave a shriek of pain and dropped his sword. Edward kicked it further away into the grass.

'Pick it up, since that will at least allow me the time to retrieve my own weapon,' he ordered. 'You will then be dealing with an opposing swordsman, and not the sort of helpless victim that you seem to prefer.'

Edward was calculating that Dempsey would instinctively revert to using his favoured sword arm — the one that had been severely weakened during his encounter with Francis some days previously. His guess proved to be correct as Dempsey leapt at him with an outraged roar, swinging his sword wildly in what looked like an attempt to hack Edward's head clean off his shoulders, as he had probably done to one of the Tower guards during the ambush at Costock.

As he came within a foot of Edward, and the blade began to whirl sideways, Edward stepped quickly to one side, causing Dempsey to lose his balance. Edward placed a foot behind him, then rammed his sword hilt into the man's exposed belly. The air seemed to leave his body as he fell backwards into the grass. Edward then stomped heavily on Dempsey's chest, while resting his sword point on his exposed throat.

'Yield, or this goes through your poxy gullet!' Edward yelled as a red rage rose before his eyes, and he silently urged Dempsey to defy him. He was called back to reality by Farnham ordering Dempsey to yield.

'I cannot afford to lose fighting men, even if they are only half decently trained,' he complained, 'so as your second in this unequal contest, I admit defeat on your behalf.'

Edward took several deep breaths to bring his heart rate back down, and in order to suppress a bloodlust that he had never experienced before. Then he slowly lifted his sword point from Dempsey's throat and stepped back warily. Dempsey glared up at him, then got awkwardly to his feet. An ominous silence followed.

'Now that sanity has been restored,' Farnham said after a few seconds, 'I think you can all see the wisdom of my choice of Master Marshall as your sword trainer. But there is need for the air to cool, so I suggest that we adjourn for an early dinner, and regather here once the sun has begun to switch to the west.'

The men filed past with downcast heads. Dempsey was the last of them. He stopped as he reached Edward, and glowered down at him from his superior height. His unkempt beard quivered with rage, and he spat at the ground within inches of Edward's feet.

'You would not have bested me had that ill-mannered oaf in the local alehouse not damaged my sword arm when he took unfair advantage of me,' Dempsey snarled. 'Once I have restored my honour by slitting his throat and burning down his alehouse, I'll be back to demand a return bout with you!'

Edward realised with rising horror that he needed to warn Francis as a matter of urgency. As he looked back towards the house, he saw Elizabeth standing in the courtyard, looking down into the field. He hurriedly overtook Dempsey and the other men on their way into dinner, then allowed Elizabeth to throw her arms around him.

'I thought the brute was about to kill you!' she wailed as she clung to him, still trembling.

Edward whispered for silence, then urged her to listen carefully. 'That oaf was never a match for me, but he has vowed to return to the inn and burn it down after killing Francis. You must lose no time in riding out of here to warn him!'

'I am supposed to be helping Margaret to prepare dinner,' she objected.

Edward grasped her by both shoulders and looked into her eyes. 'We are all but finished here anyway, since I have enough evidence to justify calling in the castle troops. Tell Francis to ride without pause in order to bring them down here. Go — now!'

Elizabeth turned on her heel and ran to the stables, where she saddled her mount faster than she had ever done, and slipped urgently onto its back. She came trotting down the courtyard at an even pace, then smiled and blew a kiss in Edward's direction as she passed him. Edward froze as he heard a familiar voice behind him.

'Where's *she* going in such a hurry?' Dempsey demanded.

Edward replied with the first thing that came into his head. 'Mistress Strong has sent her to the village for more victuals for our dinner.'

Dempsey glared back at him suspiciously, then sneered. 'She should be there in time to view the blaze, then. I will eat with more eagerness when I have killed the rat that lives inside the inn we are about to put to the torch. Then I shall escort your woman back here, persuading her as we ride that she would be better off placing her trust in a man who does not hesitate to kill when the opportunity presents itself. Out of my way, weakling, while I lead my men into battle.'

To Edward's horror, as Dempsey leapt into the saddle he was joined by four more of his followers, who had just led their horses from the stables. As they cantered out towards the gates, Edward was left with little option — he had to follow them with all speed, since he now stood to lose *two* people very dear to his heart.

13

'Why are you following us?' Dempsey demanded as Edward thundered up behind the group of five heading for the village.

'I thought I'd become a member of your armed band,' Edward asserted as he adopted the tone of a man determined to prove his worth.

Dempsey grunted dismissively. 'I don't need your help to put a serving man in his place.'

'The same serving man who disarmed you last time?' Edward challenged him. 'And if you don't need any assistance, why are these other four riding with you? For all you know, there are others at the inn who will seek to thwart your plans, so the more the merrier, surely?'

There was no reply as they swung right at the gateway to the Farnham estate and headed north. The village soon came into sight, with the modest inn at its centre, and Edward prayed hard that Elizabeth had reached it in time to warn Francis and then make her escape.

With a sinking heart, Edward noted that Elizabeth's horse was still tied to the post outside the inn. He lost no time in hitching his own mount next to it, then raced in behind Dempsey and his followers. As he reached the entrance to the main room, which fortunately was empty of customers, he saw Francis making a run for the kitchen door to the rear, and heard Dempsey calling for two of his men to follow him and bring him back securely tied. The men did as they were urged and disappeared from sight. Ten seconds later, Edward and Dempsey heard angry voices, followed by a shriek of agony from somewhere in the kitchen recesses. One of Dempsey's men staggered back into the main room clutching his eyes, from which blood was pouring.

'The bastard killed Romsey!' the man shrieked before colliding with the doorframe and falling back. He landed in the sawdust on the floor, which rapidly turned dark as it was soaked by his blood.

'After him!' Dempsey yelled to the remaining two. They raced outside, but soon returned to advise their leader that the man they were seeking had become a cloud of dust on the road north.

'We can still put the place to the torch!' Dempsey raged. 'Someone bring me a burning brand, quickly!' He stopped as he suddenly spotted Elizabeth trying to sneak out through the back door that led to the arbour. 'You! I was told that you were seeking victuals for our dinner, but it would seem that you preferred to visit the inn and cavort with that yaldson who escaped my clutches. You no doubt warned him of our intended visit! You'll pay for that by dying in the flames, to burn the lust from your soul.' He turned to grin sadistically at Edward, who was only a few paces behind him. 'And your man here can be the one to secure the ropes that will bind you to the timbers as they roast. See to it, Marshall — you can repay her cuckolding of you by watching her writhe on the pyre.'

Edward hung back, assessing the best way to proceed.

Dempsey grew angry at his hesitation. 'As I thought,' he growled, 'the man has no stomach when it comes to the shedding of blood. You two — grab the wench and secure her to that main beam, then find me a brand to send this place to perdition.'

Before the men could carry out the command, Edward drew his knife from his belt and leaped forward to throw his left arm around Dempsey's neck in a stranglehold. His right hand pushed the knife point into his throat, drawing a few drops of blood.

'Let the woman be, else your leader here will be singing through a hole in his gullet!' Edward roared.

To his intense relief, the two men froze where they stood, and Edward smiled as convincingly as he could at Elizabeth.

'If you would be so good, my dear, as to go out through the front door and unhitch both your horse and mine, you may then take to your saddle and hold my mount in readiness for our departure. But first you may release the other horses to let them wander in search of pasture, after untying and discarding their saddle leathers.' He transferred his attention to Dempsey's two henchmen. 'As for you two, one move by either of you to hinder those instructions and your scrofulous leader will have his throat cut from ear to ear. Believe me when I say that I would be most appreciative of the excuse. So, let us about our business.'

Elizabeth ran, white-faced, across the room and out through the front door, while Edward edged in the same direction, his knife still at Dempsey's throat. Dempsey's two remaining associates stepped to one side, and Edward and his captive were able to watch from the doorway as Elizabeth followed Edward's instructions to the letter. The mounts that had brought the others from the Farnham estate trotted eagerly across the road to feed on the grass growing there once the saddles they had borne were lying in the dust. Elizabeth jumped into her own saddle as she held Edward's horse by its halter and led it towards the group in the doorway.

It was now or never. Tempting though it was to sink the knife into Dempsey's throat, Edward persuaded himself that he was a better man than that. He released the knife, then in an instant leaped back in front of his prisoner and launched a determined kick at his groin with the toe of his riding boot. Dempsey gave a howl of tortured rage as he doubled over, and Edward jumped into the saddle of the waiting horse. He yelled for Elizabeth to join him, and together they cantered out of the village, heading south in the second cloud of dust that it had witnessed that morning.

'Where are we heading?' Elizabeth enquired breathlessly as she held onto the reins.

'No idea,' Edward replied, 'but clearly we cannot head back towards Nottingham, because there is a good chance that when those oafs finally retrieve their horses, they will set off in pursuit of Francis. If they choose instead to pursue us, that will be all to the good, since it will enable Francis to reach Nottingham without hindrance. But now we must find somewhere to hide until we can somehow calculate that it is safe to return to the Farnham estate, and meet up with Burghley's men. Tell me, have you ever ridden a horse in the manner of a man, with your legs astride it? And if so, do you think that you could thereby increase the speed of your travel?'

'I used to ride in that manner as a girl on the Ashby estate, whenever I was assured that my parents were not looking. But in those days I was not wearing a heavy gown, and neither did my horse carry a sideways saddle.'

'All to the good,' Edward replied as the entrance to the Farnham estate came into view once more. 'We will halt here briefly, and cast your saddle into the grass just inside the gateway. This may serve to dupe anyone following us into believing that we have headed back towards the house, or perhaps that you fell from your horse and were injured. Either way, it will afford us the additional time to make our way further south and acquire a place in which to hide.'

'And my gown?' Elizabeth asked testily. 'Is it your intention that I ride in only my shift, or perhaps not even that? That I ape the antics of that lady in Coventry who rode naked through the streets?'

Edward chuckled. 'That would indeed be a rare sight, and one that I, for one, would applaud. But I had in mind that you hitch your gown to your waist, thus freeing your legs to grip the horse's sides when we quicken our pace. Here is the entrance, so let us lose no time.'

Elizabeth proved to be adept at riding astride her mount, and they were able to urge their horses into a fast canter as they hurried down the road that led towards distant Leicester. That had been Edward's original intended destination; however, less than thirty minutes later they passed an old stone at the side of the track that advised them that the county town was a further ten miles down the road, but that they were approaching the village of Mountsorrel. Edward laughed.

'This is the place for which I was named. I was found here as an abandoned baby, and for that reason I was given that name when they took me in at the orphanage. And unless I am mistaken, there is the very doorway in which I was abandoned.'

He nodded to their right, where the belfry tower of an ancient church stood tall beyond a stand of trees that hid the rest of the building from view. At his suggestion they urged their horses towards it, and passed through the copse of trees until they found themselves contemplating an old oaken doorway just beyond the lychgate that led into an old cemetery with a dozen or more gravestones.

In his mind, Edward conjured up an image of himself as a mewling infant lying in a basket. He had been discovered by a priest who called to open the church ahead of Evensong, then took the precious bundle south to Wigton, close by the ancient city of Leicester. He was scarcely aware that Elizabeth had dismounted as she sought to ease her aching thighs, ahead of scuttling back into the copse to answer the call of nature. Edward had dismounted himself by the time she returned and had tethered their horses to the trees, out of sight of the road.

'You can have no memory of this place, surely. Should we not be resuming our flight, if we are to evade anyone who may be pursuing us?' she asked.

Edward smiled and turned to kiss the top of her head. 'This place once served me well, and it shall do so again. Why should we not seek sanctuary here for a day or so, until those who may have followed us have given up? We may then make a dash for home, using a different route.'

'Isn't there some ancient law that says that once we claim sanctuary in there, we cannot be pursued anyway?' she asked.

'That is said to be true for common criminals pursued by officers of the law such as myself, but to be perfectly truthful I have always ignored it when I could grab the collar of some ne'er-do-well I had been chasing. And as for the likes of Dempsey and his murdering brutes, I doubt that the sanctity of a house of God would serve to divert them from their evil designs. We may, however, find that within the ancient folds of this fine church there is some corner in which we may skulk until the hue and cry abates.'

'Will the door be unlocked?'

'Such is the tradition,' Edward advised her. 'My orphanage was attached to a charity poorhouse run by monks, so I know something of church ways. One of their customs was to always leave a door unlocked, to allow parishioners to enter and worship God at any time of day or night. But that was in the old days, when folk took their religion more seriously, and the realm was not so bedevilled by thieves and vagabonds. But there is only one way to answer your question.'

The old wood creaked and groaned as they lifted the latch and peered inside the cool, dark cavern of the parish church. They stood just inside the door until their eyes adjusted to the gloom, and Edward looked upwards with a smile.

'Up there,' he said, nodding. 'Follow me.'

The building was seemingly empty of either worshippers or clergymen as they slid silently down the centre aisle to the side of the altar, where a small door was set into the right-hand wall. This also yielded to their enquiring hands, and they began to mount a rickety staircase that presumably led to the belfry above. After four turns to their right on the spiral stairs, Edward muttered with satisfaction as he spotted the tell-tale hatch that was located on the inner left wall. He pushed it open, inviting Elizabeth to go in ahead. She shrieked as a scuttling noise announced that they had startled a family of rats.

Edward tutted. 'It is either the company of God's own creatures, who are more scared of us than we should be of them, or we go back outside and expose ourselves to those spawns of Satan who would slit our throats. Your choice, but I shall remain here.'

'Where are we?' Elizabeth whispered fearfully.

'My guess is that it was the mason's loft, where those who designed and built this church laid out their templates and traced their plans in the wet plaster of the floor. There is insufficient light, but had we the means of investigating, I think we would find the faint remains of their tracings in the surface of this floor, which you will note is laid with plaster over the bare wood.'

'You are clearly knowledgeable in the matter of church history,' she replied sarcastically, 'but if it is your intention that we skulk in here for several days, do you know anything about hunting for food in the roof of a draughty old church? Or was it your intention that we chase down rats and eat them raw?'

'We are, for the moment, safe from pursuit, and therefore still alive,' said Edward. 'The matter of food and drink must be of lesser importance until we reach the point of starvation. For the time being, let us find such comfort as we can on this bare floor.'

They lay there for a while, gazing into the semi-darkness and listening to the old timbers creaking as the heat of the day came and went. Elizabeth's ears were more closely attuned to what she dreaded would be the scuttling sounds of returning rats, and so it was she who first detected the sound of movement below them. She grabbed Edward's arm and whispered hoarsely, 'There's someone down there!'

Edward soon picked up the sound of outdoor footwear on old flagstones, and wriggled carefully across the floor until he found a point at which the plaster appeared thinner. He tested it with his hand, then drawing the knife from his belt, he scraped away until he was down to the original floorboard and began digging into it. The old wood posed little resistance, and soon he had a peephole that looked down directly on the altar below, where he could just make out the shape of a person — it could have been either a man or a woman — lighting a candle on the altar and leaving a small posy of flowers beside it. A short while later, heavier footsteps preceded the sight of a man kneeling in front of the altar in prayer, before the sounds from below indicated that Evensong was being celebrated.

As darkness fell, Elizabeth nestled close to Edward for warmth, and told him that she was tired, hungry, frightened and needing to empty her bladder.

'Over there in the corner,' he advised her, 'then join me back here, so that we can keep warm,' he said with a smile.

An hour later, they lay listening to the rising wind that was rattling through the worn masonry. Then there were stealthy footsteps in the church below them, and Elizabeth grabbed Edward's arm again in fear. 'Are places like this not said to be haunted by the spirits of those who have passed on?' she whispered with a tremble on her lips.

Edward listened as intently as he could. 'Did you ever hear of a ghost with shortness of breath?'

'If they be true ghosts,' Elizabeth whispered back, 'then surely they have no breath at all.'

'Precisely,' he replied, 'which is why whoever is below us is no ghost. But what they are doing here at this late hour is another matter. Remain still.'

He rolled over to the approximate location of the peephole he had created, then scrabbled around with his hand until he found it, pressing his eye to the opening. There was a moon of sorts that night, casting a grey glow over the altar area of the church. He froze as he spotted a hooded figure bending over the altar as if in prayer, before rising back upright, making the sign of the cross, then backing away from his line of sight. But something had been left on the altar — something he could not identify, but which he would examine further at first light.

When he did so, he uttered a faint hiss of surprise that was sufficient to alert Elizabeth, who had slept fitfully with dreams of ghostly rats.

'What?' she demanded.

'It looks as if someone has left us some food!' Edward announced gleefully.

Elizabeth frowned. 'I used to kill rats by leaving food out for them before I despatched them with my broom. I suspect that this is a similar trap.'

'It may be,' Edward conceded, 'but this is a house of God, remember. I have been saved once by the Christian charity that resides within the breasts of many clergymen — even our present ones. It may be that some kindly priest has become aware of our predicament and left us the means of survival. Either way, I cannot lie here knowing that there is food below, but doing nothing to acquire it. So — trap or no trap — here I go. You should remain silent and hidden, in case I am taken as I reach for it.'

He came back shortly afterwards, carrying a basket laden with bread, salted fish, a portion of cold lamb and a corked container of small beer. As they began to eat, Elizabeth looked into the bottom of the basket and extracted a piece of parchment with writing on it. She cleared her mouth and read it aloud. 'Leave the empty basket where you found it. There will be more tomorrow.'

'Hardly the actions of someone seeking to ensnare us,' Edward commented. 'Let us hope that the promise is fulfilled.'

It was indeed, that night and the following night. No longer hungry or fearful of discovery, they grew inquisitive regarding their secret benefactor. Edward agreed that the following night he would conceal himself in the doorway of the belfry stairs that lay to the side of the altar and keep watch. Elizabeth insisted on keeping additional watch through their spyhole, in case it was after all a trap and Edward was captured. If this was the case, she would ride alone towards Nottingham, in the hope that Francis was by now returning with the castle troops.

Edward was just beginning to fear that either the promise had somehow been broken, or their unknown patron had been discovered on their way, when he heard the creaking of the front door of the church, and a soft footfall on the flagstones. The shadowy shape flitted alongside his hiding place, then bent to lay something on the altar. He pounced and grabbed the surprisingly frail figure around the waist.

He turned them round sharply, causing the hood to fall back, then gasped as he recognised the thin face of Margaret Strong.

'You!' he said in amazement. 'What business is it of yours to be bringing us food and drink when we are running from your employer?'

'He is only my employer,' Margaret replied, 'and I do not owe him what I owe to you after all these years. And if a woman may not save her own son from starvation, then what sort of a world has it become?'

14

Edward stood there, open-mouthed and with his eyes bulging. Elizabeth slipped down the narrow staircase to join him.

'How? When? I mean … what…?' Edward stammered.

Elizabeth took his arm in a gesture of support. 'I think what my husband means is, how do you know?'

Margaret smiled. 'I knew the minute I laid eyes on him, when you both first arrived at Nether Hall. You are the living image of your father, Edward, and I nearly swooned with the shock of seeing him again — that is, you in his likeness. Then Elizabeth confirmed the year in which you were born, and the fact that you had been an orphan abandoned in a church doorway. That confirmed what I already knew in my heart. Would you like to meet the man who took you to that orphanage in Wigston?'

'Is my father still alive?' Edward croaked.

Margaret shook her head sadly. 'He died of the sweating sickness some years ago. But you can still pay your respects to him, because his grave is in this churchyard. It is well cared for, and the name is still legible on the memorial stone. But the man who took you to the orphanage lives next door to this church.'

'The house next door is the parsonage, is it not?' Elizabeth put in. 'I believe I saw a man dressed like a parson tending a grave in the churchyard when we were tethering our horses to those trees out there.'

'A parson does indeed live in the adjoining house,' Margaret confirmed. 'He is my brother, and he is expecting us.'

'Will it be safe for us to break from our cover?' asked Edward.

'Do you think your own uncle — a man of the cloth — would betray you?' Margaret demanded. 'He has known of your presence here ever since he saw you scuttling in, believing that you had not been seen. Yet he has only made your presence known to me, and may therefore be trusted. Or would you prefer to remain in that draughty loft?'

'Of course not, and please excuse my ingratitude, but I have suddenly been given so much information to absorb,' Edward apologised. 'There is nothing to keep us here, and I feel sure that a welcoming hearth would be as much appreciated by Elizabeth as by myself. So please lead the way.'

'I will once you have embraced me in the manner appropriate for a son with his mother,' Margaret smiled as she held her arms out. 'I have waited many long years for this, and that last embrace left something to be desired, given that it was intended to capture me like some burglar caught in the act.'

Edward hugged her and tears ran down both their faces. Elizabeth was forced to look away before she gave way to her own emotions.

The three of them scurried to the parsonage as some clouds briefly obscured the moonlight. A grey-haired man opened the door.

'Welcome home at long last!' he greeted as he hugged Edward. 'And this must be your wife, of whom Margaret speaks so highly. Come inside, and sit close to the fire. I keep it lit even during the summer months. My bones grow cold and brittle with the passing years, I'm afraid, and I grow weaker with time.'

'Let's at least eat some of this food,' Margaret said as she placed her basket on the table in the small, all-purpose room.

'Your Uncle Richard can say grace before we eat, but only after he warms up some of his excellent pumpkin stew. I may be a housekeeper, but Richard was always the better pupil when our mother taught us to cook. Your grandmother of course, Edward, and she too may be found in the churchyard these many years.'

'I'm told that it was you who carried me to that orphanage,' Edward smiled at Richard as they partook of their meal. 'I suppose I must apologise for my ingratitude in escaping from there when I was fifteen.'

'Not at all,' said Richard, 'since I am informed by Margaret that you have made a good life, and were once a soldier. It is to our queen's discredit that so many of your ilk are forced to wander the countryside begging, but you seem to be better than that.'

'Indeed he is,' Elizabeth assured him. 'He is bailiff to the Sheriff of Nottinghamshire.'

'Then why is he in Leicestershire?' Margaret enquired. 'I sensed that his true purpose in presenting at Nether Hall was far from desiring to become a posturing fool like Marlowe.'

'I will tell all once you have answered all the questions that are currently burning a hole in my head,' Edward promised. 'Who was my father, how did he live, how did he die, and why?'

It fell silent as Richard and Margaret exchanged uncomfortable glances. Margaret cleared her throat to answer.

'Since the sin was mine, it must fall to me to answer for your orphan status.'

'It was sin that led to my birth?' Edward enquired, somewhat taken aback.

Margaret nodded. 'Most would have called it sin, but you were born out of love, Edward. I never gave you a name, but I am glad that you adopted such a noble one, and one that many of our former kings were known by.'

'I did not choose it,' Edward advised her. 'It was the name given to me in the orphanage. May I assume that I was carried there because you could not keep me? I was born out of wedlock, presumably?'

'Yes, you were, but … well, you must believe me when I say how … that is…'

Her words became lost in choking sobs, and Richard put his arm across her shoulder.

'You must allow me to continue with the tale,' he said quietly. 'Your father was a boyhood friend of mine, Edward. His name was Robert Sangster, and he and I attended the same seminary attached to Leicester Abbey in the final days before its closure. I went on to finish my studies elsewhere and was eventually ordained. Then I was presented to this living by the Cavendish family, who then owned most of the land in this part of the county, including that upon which the old abbey once stood. Meanwhile, Robert wandered from one remaining holy house to another until he finally became ordained as a priest in the old religion. Then the purges began in the reign of Edward, and he was obliged to go into hiding. He remained a fugitive until Mary came to the throne, and he was once again free to conduct Masses in the old way.'

'It must have been a most turbulent period,' Edward acknowledged, 'and I can recall for myself some of the older monks in my orphanage who had taken to a life of charity in order to retain a roof over their own heads. They spoke in awe of those who had remained true to their vocation, and still preached wherever they could find a congregation. I had no idea that my father had been one of them. Presumably he eventually called here?'

'Yes, indeed he did,' Richard recalled. 'He arrived here one day, half-starved and very frightened that the new regime of Elizabeth, despite the assurances she gave, would seek him out and put him to death. So he lived here like our brother, since Margaret had become my housekeeper following the death of our mother. She and Robert became very close — as it turned out, *too* close.'

'Thank you, Richard,' Margaret interposed, 'I think that I should at least take responsibility for explaining the next part to Edward.' She leaned across the table to take his hand. 'Since you have known the carnal love of a woman, you can perhaps appreciate how the fires of temptation burned. What happened between us on occasions when Richard was absent from the house was of course a wicked sin before God, but it also brought the most blissful happiness I have ever known. You were born of that bliss, and you must believe me when I assure you that it was true love such as I cannot fully describe.'

'You have no need,' Edward replied as tears welled in his eyes and he gripped her hand more tightly, 'since I have found the same with Elizabeth. I give thanks that I was not the outcome of some foolish tumble in a hayrick after too much ale. But I can well imagine the dilemma when you learned that you were carrying me.'

'Indeed, and all three of us talked long and hard about what was to be done. In the end Robert took it upon himself to depart from the house. Even now, I become almost bereft of reason when I recall the day that I saw him walking the road back to Leicester. He had everything he possessed wrapped in a small sack over his shoulder, along with enough food to last him for no more than three days. Oh dear God, I still cannot bear the memory!'

She began wailing, and a tear-stained Elizabeth rushed around the table to hold her tightly. Edward gazed helplessly across the table at Richard, who continued the tale.

'When he had left, we agreed that there was only one thing we could do once you were born. A kindly local woman with five of her own acted as midwife, and we swore her to a holy vow of silence. I then took you to the orphanage when you were barely two months old, and had proved that you could tolerate broth instead of mother's milk. To put paid to any possible gossip, Margaret sought employment as a housemaid on the Farnham estate and eventually worked her way up to become the housekeeper of Nether Hall.'

'And my father?' Edward enquired. 'What became of him?'

Richard's face fell. 'Some six years ago, a group of my parishioners came to my door one winter's night to tell me that there was a man lying in a ditch by the side of the Leicester track. He appeared to be very ill, and was calling for either me or Margaret. I hurried over, and there was Robert in the final stages of the sweating sickness. I brought him home and made him as comfortable as I could, but I was unable to give him news of either you or Margaret, which he begged for. He died later that night, and we buried him in the churchyard out there.'

Edward dabbed at the tear that rolled down his face. 'At least I can still pay my respects at his headstone. I can only hope that he's proud of me from where he looks down on my daily activities.'

'Which you have so far avoided disclosing,' Margaret reminded him. 'It was no accident that you called at Nether Hall, was it?'

Edward sighed and shook his head. 'Indeed not, but you must know that you have been playing host to some very vicious and dangerous men.'

'Of this I am already aware,' said Margaret, 'but I am not the host. Neither, really, is my master Sir Ralph, since these men arrived unbidden and unexpectedly when we had thought to host only one. He is a man you have not seen, despite having been in residence at the hall for some days. He is being kept hidden away in a secret chamber concealed within the roof timbers, and comes out only to conduct Masses.'

'I have actually seen him,' said Edward. 'I crept into the minstrel gallery of the great hall to find out what was transpiring on the day that you had Elizabeth's assistance, and she learned of the portraits that exist on both sides of the picture frames. But when, and under what circumstances, did the others arrive, pray?'

Margaret grimaced. 'The first of them was that awful man Marlowe. He told the master that he was travelling the country with a group of players, and would be delighted to put on several of his tragedies for the amusement of the household and any guests we might have. There were only four of them to begin with, but not long after the players arrived a further five or six rode in, heavily armed and looking as if they had been on the road for several weeks. Sir Ralph seemed delighted to receive them, and they had been there for almost a week when you arrived.'

'So this second group of men — the ones who were heavily armed — they arrived separately from Master Marlowe's small company?' Edward enquired eagerly.

'So it appeared, but they blended in with each other so easily that I formed the distinct belief that they already knew each other, and that their coming together was no coincidence.

Certainly the master seemed to know them, and was only too happy to be invited to supervise their training. But what are they being trained *for*? Do you happen to know?'

'I think I do,' said Edward, 'and I can give you more intelligence regarding their true purpose. You must forgive me for my deception when I sought hospitality under your roof, but I had been sent there by the queen's secretary, Baron Burghley.'

'You work for Her Majesty?' Margaret asked, clearly impressed.

'Not directly, but my master is the Sheriff of Nottinghamshire, and I am his bailiff. Between us we are responsible for the preservation of the Queen's Peace in Nottinghamshire.'

'But this is Leicestershire,' said Margaret.

'Indeed, but I have been sent to investigate the activities of these men whom your master has been training because they are suspected of having killed four people in my county, two of them in the town proper. Two of those four victims were justices, and it is believed that these men are intended to be part of a larger force that will rise up in rebellion in order to place on the throne a young lady called Arbella Stuart. She is a staunch Catholic, and an alternative claimant to the English Crown to James of Scotland. If they strike in Her Majesty's lifetime they will clearly be guilty of treason, but it was my task to prevent that from happening by identifying where they were hiding, what was their true business, and whether or not they might be taken up for the four murders to which I have already referred.'

Margaret sat for a moment, taking all this in, then looked pleadingly at Richard. 'I hope that what you have heard does not loosen your resolve to harbour your nephew and his wife as you promised me you would. Should their true identities be revealed to those ruffians in Nether Hall, they would be cruelly done to death.'

'Surely our true identities are already known to them?' Edward argued.

Margaret looked uncertain. 'Of that I cannot be sure. I know that the ruffian Dempsey, who seems to be the leader of the armed group, is seeking your head for interfering with some scheme he had to seek revenge against a man residing at the inn in Quorndon, but beyond that he has said nothing.'

'The man to whom you refer — the one at the inn,' Edward began, 'is a colleague and good friend of mine called Francis Barton. He is bailiff to the Sheriff of Nottingham — the town itself, as distinct from the county — and hopefully he has safely returned to Nottingham with the news I had to impart regarding my suspicions against Dempsey and his followers. There is a contingent of soldiers from the Tower of London barracked in the castle, and they will be brought south immediately to take custody of your house guests ahead of their arrest and transportation down to London. If we are to stay here in hiding and you are to remain at Nether Hall, could you undertake to travel down here to advise us when they arrive? We will then know when it is safe for us to journey back to Nether Hall.'

'Of course, but will the soldiers from Nottingham not make me a prisoner also, in the belief that I am party to whatever evil schemes have been devised?'

'She has a good point, Edward,' Elizabeth agreed. 'We ourselves had no reason to believe that Margaret was not in league with the plotters, so how will Francis know that she can be trusted?'

'I have two answers to that,' Edward replied. 'The first is that I write a brief note to Francis, advising him that Margaret is my mother, and can be trusted to journey a few miles in order to bring us back to Nether Hall. The other is that she simply advises Francis where we may be found, and he can then come and relieve us. The choice is yours, Mother — which would you prefer?'

Margaret thought for a moment, then smiled broadly. 'We have waited so long to be reunited that we should take every opportunity to be together, I feel. I propose that I continue to ride down here every day, as I have been doing with your food baskets, on the pretence of bringing sustenance to my brother. On the final occasion I shall return with this Francis of whom you speak, and we may then all ride back together.'

Richard brought vellum, ink and a quill, and Edward wrote a short note addressed to Francis, which Margaret tucked into a fold of her gown. As she departed, there were tearful hugs and exchanges of loving endearments between mother and son. Then Richard insisted that Edward and Elizabeth enjoy a comfortable bed after their privations in the mason's loft in the church next door, and he gave up his chamber in order to sleep by the fire in the main room.

The following day, Edward spent his time removing a few stray weeds and encroaching grass from his father's grave. The headstone read: *Robert Sangster, 1540–1583, beloved friend of Richard and Margaret, now at peace in the arms of God.* Elizabeth watched him sadly, but kept one eye on the track from Quorndon that was just visible through the trees. Margaret duly arrived as the sun was sinking to the west behind the rear garden of the parsonage, and as they sat down to a hearty supper she was able to advise them that as yet there was no sign of Francis and the soldiers from Nottingham.

The same happened on the following two days, and Edward was growing anxious.

'They should have arrived by now,' he said nervously to Elizabeth as they sat under the parsonage front porch, enjoying the late sunset on the fourth day.

'Perhaps the castle contingent were engaged with other exercises,' she said, sounding unconvinced.

Edward shook his head. 'They had instructions to hold themselves in readiness for Francis to collect them and bring them south, so they would have headed out as soon as he summoned them. My fear is that something may have happened to Francis. And Mother is late this afternoon.'

'You seem to have become altogether more nervous since you have been reunited with your mother,' Elizabeth said as she leaned across to kiss him.

Edward grinned. 'Well, becoming a dutiful son with a mother to care about after all these years is inclined to take the recklessness out of you. And I'm hungry. Until Mother arrives with her food basket, we have nothing for supper.'

'I believe I saw Richard harvesting some more pumpkins from his vegetable patch earlier today, and there's some bread left over from dinner, so we won't starve. Being a "dutiful son" has also improved your appetite, and I do believe that I can see your belly beginning to peep out over your tunic belt.'

Despite all of Elizabeth's efforts to restore the flagging spirits of the two men, it was a gloomy supper for the three of them, with the vacant seat normally occupied by Margaret all too obvious.

The following morning, when the crowing of a distant cockerel woke Elizabeth, she rolled over to find that Edward was missing. She found him sitting in the front porch, looking dolefully north.

'You can't sit here all day, staring at an empty track,' she chided. 'Come inside and have some bread, at least.'

He allowed himself to be led indoors, where he accepted a slice of slightly stale black bread dipped in the dripping from Richard's basting tray, then wandered back outside. Richard came in from the main room in which he had been sleeping ever since his house guests had arrived, and shook his head sadly.

'If Margaret fails to return to us today, I fear that your husband will foolishly ride back to Quorndon in search of her, which would imperil them both,' he confided to Elizabeth.

'I think that Edward has more sense than that,' Elizabeth replied, then cocked her ear when she heard Edward's shout from the front door.

'Here they come! God be praised, here they come!'

He ran heedlessly through the copse of trees that lay between the track and the church, in which their horses were still tethered, and burst out into the open. He was greeted by a rousing cheer from Francis and a cry of welcome from Margaret, who was riding at his side. They dismounted together and embraced Edward, apologising for their failure to arrive the previous day.

'We took a little while to round them all up, since they scattered when they saw us arrive,' Francis explained breathlessly. 'We have all the rest, I believe, but there is no sign of the large hairy one who twice tried to kill me. Did you put paid to him after I fled north?'

'No, it was all we could do to escape ourselves,' Edward replied, 'but the man must be found without delay, because he would seem to have been the leader of the gang of cut-throats.'

162

'There's time enough for that,' Francis reassured him. 'I sent a fast horse down to London to bring Burghley up here in order to interrogate those we have captured, and no doubt they'll tell us where the murderous ape may have gone to ground. For the moment I'm both hungry and thirsty, since we left while it was still dark.'

'Come inside and have what's left of our bread and small beer,' Edward invited him, 'and by the look of that bulging pannier on Mother's horse, there are other delights to be consumed.'

Inside the parson's house the formal introductions were made, and Margaret and Elizabeth set about opening the food parcels and laying the table ahead of the celebratory breakfast. Edward sat beside Francis, swigging from an ale pot.

'So even if Dempsey escaped, how many more of them have you secured?' he asked.

'We have seven evil-looking coves securely locked in the basement, with guards on the door. We also believe that there may be a priest hidden somewhere, since our brief search of the house revealed altar cloths, candles and other symbols of Popery. So the missing one — he of the hairy countenance — is called "Dempsey", is that so?'

'Yes,' Edward confirmed, 'and your suspicion regarding Masses being held is correct. Mother here advises me that there is a priest hidden in the roof timbers, so we may flush him out when we return. But what of Marlowe and those posing as his players? Do you hold him secure?'

Francis's face took on a troubled expression. 'The man claims some sort of immunity in Her Majesty's name. I did not take him at face value, and he is locked up separately in another chamber in the house. However, he handed me some sort of seal that he claimed was his token of royal service, and asked my man riding south to ensure that it was handed to Burghley in person. I expect the reinforcements from London to be here by the end of the week, so then we shall know the truth one way or the other.'

'Marlowe always seemed somewhat apart from the others,' Edward conceded, before changing the subject. 'Did Mother tell you the joyous story of how she and I were reunited after all these years?'

'Indeed, she has spoken of little else,' Francis said, smiling kindly across at Margaret, 'and I believe that your late father lies buried in the graveyard outside.'

'That is so,' Edward confirmed, 'so when we have all finished this fine meal, let us go out there and say a short prayer over his headstone.'

The sun was high as Edward led the way to the headstone belonging to Robert Sangster. There was a thick wood over the far side of the churchyard wall, and the cheerful sound of birdsong provided musical accompaniment to the blessing that Richard intoned for the soul of his old friend as they all bowed their heads in prayer.

Then came an ominous whirling sound, followed by a squelching thud. Margaret gave a faint cry from where she stood between Edward and Francis before pitching face first onto the grave of the man who had been her lifelong love. There was a crossbow bolt buried deep in her side, and as Francis raced out through the lychgate to retrieve his horse and give chase, Edward threw himself over his mother's body with an anguished howl.

15

Edward was sobbing like a child as Richard choked out the funeral blessing and Francis shovelled the last of the earth over the mound that would forever hide the remains of Margaret Strong. The local stonemason had already received the commission for the headstone that would record the location, and Richard could be relied upon to place flowers daily on her final resting place alongside that of Robert Sangster.

Edward was inconsolable, and had divided the remainder of the day that had followed Margaret's untimely death between fits of howling grief and bursts of white-hot anger against whoever had been responsible. Elizabeth held him tightly, whichever mood he was in, but could offer no words of consolation.

'We were separated by Fate for twenty-five years, and only allowed a few days together by that same cruel mistress of destiny,' Edward wailed. 'It's not fair! It's not right! Where was God in all this?'

Elizabeth and Francis had also been obliged to physically restrain him from leaping onto his horse and heading off in pursuit of whoever had delivered the fatal crossbow bolt. Francis had initially tried to give chase himself, and had returned with a grim face, explaining that he had failed to catch up with the person responsible. Edward seemed convinced that it had been the missing Dempsey, and had not been at all consoled by Francis's suggestion that he himself had been the target, and that Margaret had been the unfortunate victim of a poor aim. Whoever had been the real target, Edward had raged, it had been his mother who had died, and he would not rest until he had taken his revenge on whoever it had been.

For an hour or two he had been successfully diverted by the task of digging the grave, which he had insisted on doing alone. He and Richard had then mournfully wrapped Margaret's body in the best shroud they could find — a former altar cloth that had been employed for the past twenty years as a screen inside the adjoining church. By the time the funeral service had ended, the sun was rapidly sinking below the trees to the west of the churchyard, from which the fatal shot had been fired. The group of four then made their mournful way back into the house.

Since Edward could not be persuaded to eat, and Elizabeth had no appetite either, the two of them made their way back into the church. Elizabeth held her arm firmly across Edward's shoulders as he prayed and cried in equal measure, and the long night ended with a pale dawn whose promise of a new day only deepened Edward's gloom.

Francis and Richard had spent the night deep in conversation, since neither of them had felt inclined to sleep. Richard's grief at the tragic loss of his sister was as strong as Edward's, and Francis found that he could console the parson by listening to his stories about Margaret's life.

'She never got over the loss of Robert Sangster,' said Richard, 'and her whole life seemed to be lived under the shadow of his departure.'

'She never thought to search for him?' Francis asked.

Richard shook his head. 'She voiced her intention of doing so, more than once, but I persuaded her that it was for the best that he be allowed to expiate his sin by continuing his work for the Lord. I have no idea where he wandered, and I did not see him again until the night that I found him in a ditch, already close to death. You have to remember that Margaret was still only sixteen years old when Robert walked away. I was her much older brother, and the one who guided our lives after our parents died.'

'And did she also mourn the loss of Edward?' Francis asked.

'Perhaps not so much as she did the loss of Robert. That does not make her less of a mother, of course. I never told her which orphanage he was placed in, in order to prevent her from seeking him out. I diverted her from her black mood by using such influence as I had to find her a position as a housemaid at Nether Hall, and she went from strength to strength in the service of the Farnham family.'

'There was no other love in her life?'

'None of which I am aware. She seemed resigned to the service of others, and on the many occasions when she visited me here our conversations were either of the past, or of her progress in domestic service.'

'How did she react to Robert's death?'

'She was strangely accepting of it. I had obviously dreaded telling her, but I had to, so that she might be present at his burial. Her only reaction was to observe that he had been dead to her all these years anyway, and that at least he could now look down upon her from Heaven. She shed no tears at his funeral, but simply placed a single red rose on his grave.'

Francis wiped a tear from his own cheek, and sought forgiveness for his weakness.

Richard smiled. 'It at least proves that you have not lost your humanity as the result of the terrible deeds you must witness, and the evil that you are called upon to suppress daily. Likewise Edward, whose human frailty has been only too obvious this past day. How will you seek to divert him from his grief?'

'I shall leave that to Elizabeth, and God be thanked that he has her by his side. She's a remarkable woman, and Edward has come to rely on her to keep him human. For myself, I think that I can keep him occupied in the business that lies ahead. There are prisoners waiting to be transported down to London for interrogation, and the men I brought with me from Nottingham to guard them are less than a dozen in number. We shall be kept busy enough, I suspect.'

'Did you plan to leave on the morrow?'

'If I can persuade Edward to accompany me, then certainly. Part of me urges that I get him back to his duties before grief curdles his brain, but another part of me advises that he needs time to grieve.'

'I have seen much grief during my years as a man of God,' said Richard, 'and it has been my experience that different people react to it in different ways. Edward strikes me as first and foremost a man of action, so it might be as well to urge him about his duties. My fear is that he will not rest until he has found this man Dempsey, whom he blames for the death of his mother, and that he will get himself killed when and if he finally hunts him down.'

'You need have no fear of that,' Francis replied grimly, 'but I shall follow both your guidance and my first thought. Tomorrow I shall drag Edward away from here by reminding him that we are both on a mission entrusted to us by the man closest to the queen — a man who will be arriving shortly at Nether Hall, and will be seeking to learn how we have acquitted ourselves.'

'Good luck with that. Now I see that we have talked our way through the night, and that the pale light to the east through yonder window heralds a new day. Would you care for some fresh bread? It would ease my mind to do something of a practical nature.'

To everyone's profound relief, Edward needed no persuasion that life had to continue. After Elizabeth had all but force-fed him two slices of bread and homemade honey, he climbed into the saddle. With a final wave and many shouted thanks to Richard for his hospitality, the three of them headed north in the direction of Quorndon. They had barely covered half a mile before Elizabeth was obliged to advise Edward that in order to ride his horse more effectively, he needed to watch the road ahead, rather than look back towards the grave they had just left.

As Nether Hall came into sight Edward seemed to acquire more of a sense of purpose, and a greater awareness of his immediate surroundings. They were met at the gate by the Captain of the Nottingham Castle Guard, who had been assigned command of the Tower infantry brought north by Burghley some weeks previously. He raised his hand in welcome as he recognised Francis.

'Welcome back, Bailiff Barton. Is that Bailiff Mountsorrel who accompanies you?'

'It is indeed,' Edward shouted back before Francis could reply, 'and the lady who rides with me is my wife. How go your prisoners?'

'Still alive, and still imprisoned. I'm Captain Poultney, and my men have been allocated duties on a day and night basis. Hopefully we shall soon be augmented by more Tower men, then we can all relax. It would be of considerable relief to me if one or other of you would assume control of things here.'

'Leave that to me,' Francis volunteered as he raised a hand to silence Edward's protest before he even made it. 'Now, pray guide us to your makeshift prison.'

'Why you?' Edward demanded petulantly as they trotted their mounts behind that of Captain Poultney. 'These men who await Burghley killed a royal justice within my jurisdiction, so they are surely my prisoners.'

'They also killed another justice in mine,' Francis reminded him, 'not to mention a prostitute and an escaped prisoner. On numbers alone I have priority over you, and you must admit that you have become somewhat distracted by recent tragic events.'

'That was yesterday,' Edward insisted, 'and today I claim priority over you, on the grounds that the first of their brutal acts occurred in the county.'

'If you insist,' Francis concurred with a subtle wink at Elizabeth, 'then of course I must defer to you. But the first sign that you have lost your grip and I shall be obliged to step in to protect our joint interests.'

They dismounted in the courtyard, where the stable boy took the bridles and led their mounts away for a feed and a rubbing down.

'You seem to have been able to retain at least some of the servants,' Francis remarked to Captain Poultney.

'All of them, with the exception of the housekeeper,' Poultney replied. 'She disappeared two nights ago, and has probably sought something better than this crumbling ruin.'

'She has found something better indeed,' Elizabeth leaped in before Edward could descend into another grief-ridden rant regarding the murder of his mother, 'but when I was here previously, she taught me much about the ordering of the household, so I will assume those duties. You still have cooks?'

'Two of them, indifferent though they seem to be. It's perhaps a miracle that we haven't been poisoned. We also have the dubious services of several servers and housemaids, who sullenly go about their duties because, I strongly suspect, they have nowhere else to go.'

'You may also leave it to me to ensure a regular supply of edible food,' Elizabeth added. 'And now I will set about my new duties, while you three men set about the efficient supervision of your prisoners, who from memory are a disreputable bunch.'

She strode purposefully towards the house, and Captain Poultney followed her with an admiring stare. 'A truly remarkable woman, if I am permitted to say so.'

'You may,' Edward confirmed with a smile. 'Now, regarding your prisoners?'

Poultney grimaced. 'They are safely confined; that is all I can advise at this stage. The obvious cut-throats among them are locked in a cellar beneath the main building. I took the precaution of ensuring that it is not a wine cellar, then simply locked the door on them. It now stinks to high heaven in there, since they have no midden or closed stool, and have taken it upon themselves to foul the place. They are fed but once a day, and at that time the guard on the only door is doubled. I have divided my men into two groups of three, one of which guards the door during daylight hours, and the other at night, although the lack of light down there results in little difference between the two. I had hoped that each of you might assume responsibility for the supervision of each group, leaving me free, with my remaining two men, to patrol the grounds and the upper floors of the main building.'

Francis smiled at Edward. 'Since you are the one with a wife whose new-found duties will occupy her during the hours of daylight, you might wish to take the day command while I assume responsibility for the hours of darkness. If you are agreeable to this arrangement, I shall now take myself off to a suitable chamber to catch up on some sleep.'

'Before you do,' Poultney interjected, 'you should know that there are two additional detainees who cause me concern. The first is a strange man who claims that he is merely here in order to stage masques of some sort. He insists that he has Her Majesty's indemnity for his presence here, and should therefore be afforded better accommodation, and a high degree of respect for his status.'

'That sounds like Master Marlowe,' said Edward. 'Where is he confined?'

'To chambers on the first floor, guarded by one man only. He is relieved on a rotational arrangement by the other remaining guard. It would be ideal if I could release Marlowe from confinement, since it would free up two men whose services I could employ elsewhere. Yet I dare not throw him into the cellar with the others in case he truly does have the queen's favour, in which case my office would be stripped from me.'

'You must maintain the current arrangement until we are advised, one way or the other, what is to become of him,' Edward confirmed. 'Who is the other detainee of whom you speak?'

Poultney shook his head slightly. 'In truth, I do not know for certain that he exists, but if he does then he must be halfway to starvation, since there has been no direct communication with him, nor has any food been left for his sustenance. But before she took herself off, the former housekeeper advised me of a man who was being kept hidden somewhere within a secret chamber built into the roof beams. It seems that his presence here was a closely guarded matter, and that he emerged only at certain times to conduct religious services.'

'I too was advised of his presence,' Edward confirmed. 'I assume from what you tell us that no efforts have been made to confirm these rumours?'

'Indeed not. From what I have already advised you, it has perhaps become obvious that we lack the manpower to go crawling through the roof aperture like rooks seeking a roosting place. We have, however, sealed off the upper floor that gives access to the roof, so that if he exists, and regardless of where his hidden chamber may be, he is powerless to come down to ground level with a view to escape.'

'Unless we smoke him out,' Francis put in. 'If farm rats can be flushed from an empty grain store with smoking brands, why not a Catholic priest?'

'Can you arrange a suitable quantity of smoke?' Poultney asked.

Francis's grin widened. 'I can once the place is on fire.'

In the ensuing silence, both men uncomfortably considered the implications of what was being suggested.

'You propose to put the house to the torch?' Edward enquired, aghast. When Francis nodded, Edward shook his head. 'You forget that we all rely on the main building for our own bodily comfort, and for the housing of our prisoners. If Burghley returns to find that we have burned the place to the ground, thereby depriving him of prisoners to put to the question, we will ourselves become candidates for the headsman on Tower Hill.'

'Do you have a better suggestion?' Francis challenged him.

Edward nodded vigorously. 'Indeed I do.' He turned to Poultney. 'What have you done with Sir Ralph Farnham, the lord of this ancient pile? Or did he escape?'

'He is allowed a more genteel confinement within his own private chambers,' Poultney advised him. 'He gave his word as a knight of the realm that he would not seek to escape, and besides, he is a somewhat elderly man who seems incapable of even climbing onto a horse, and even less of making his escape at a gallop.'

'Take me to him,' Edward commanded, then turned to Francis. 'Go and sleep, and then you and I will further consider your proposal over supper.'

Edward was led to Ralph Farnham's private chamber.

'I wondered when we might anticipate your return,' said Farnham, smiling with resignation as Edward entered the room. 'I should have appreciated that there was more about you than the average wandering vagabond who had once seen service under the Crown. They tell me that you have summoned Baron Burghley, who will no doubt, in due course, accept my reasons for having given hospitality to the wrong sort of person.'

'If I might anticipate those reasons,' Edward put in, 'I believe you have never given up your Catholic faith, and have for many years succeeded in maintaining your estate as one upon which Masses might be conducted in secret. You were persuaded, perhaps by Marlowe, to give sanctuary to someone who is highly regarded by Rome, and whose piety and closeness to God was too much of a temptation for you to resist. Then this same man prevailed upon you to extend your hospitality to a more warlike bunch who consider themselves "Soldiers for Christ", and who are pledged to restore a Catholic to the throne of England. What you did not appreciate, until it was too late, was that the replacement of a Protestant monarch by a Catholic one was planned to occur before the natural death of the former.'

Farnham nodded sadly. 'You have it in a nutshell. I am but a foolish old man, and shall no doubt pay for it with the loss of my estate, and possibly my head. But at least I shall meet my maker with my soul untarnished.'

'Even if you allow your illustrious priestly guest to be burned alive?' Edward enquired.

Farnham's mouth dropped open in horror. 'You have found him, and now intend to burn him at the stake?'

'Neither, as yet. But others of my acquaintance, rather than seek out his place of hiding, intend to put the brand to the top floor of your manor house in an effort to smoke him out. If you have had experience of how flames can take effect on a wooden house frame covered in old thatch, then you will appreciate that whoever you are hiding up there will have little practical hope of escape from the flames.'

'You come to me because you believe I can prevent such a terrible act?'

'*Only* you, I believe. Only you can persuade him that it would be better for him to surrender himself now, rather than roast alive as a prelude to going to his grave unshriven.'

'Dear God,' Farnham muttered, 'was ever a man exposed to such a dilemma?'

'There is no dilemma, Sir Ralph,' Edward insisted. 'In your hands lies the life of a priest of your chosen faith, and on your conscience would lie his death. I shall leave you to contemplate your options, and shall return in the forenoon tomorrow to learn of your response.'

Over supper, Edward told Francis what had passed.

'Do you think he will comply?' Francis asked.

Edward shrugged. 'I know I would, but who can tell? At least, if he does not, then your conscience will be the clearer.'

'You are assuming that I possess one,' said Francis. 'And you forget that this priest in the rafters was the inspiration and counsellor of those whose wickedness led to the death of your mother.'

Elizabeth gasped and glared at Francis. 'For shame, Francis!' she upbraided him. 'I had just begun to hope that the wound was starting to heal.'

'It will *never* heal!' Edward yelled as he rose to his feet and swept his platter from the supper table. 'Nor will I eat until I have cornered Dempsey and run him through for his evil!'

'You will never find him, Edward, so resume your seat and eat something,' Francis urged him.

Edward was halfway out of the door as he turned and bellowed back, 'I shall prove you wrong there, Francis!'

Furious, Elizabeth turned to Francis. 'See what you have done?' she cried. 'He has not slept for two days, and now he races after a dangerous murderer armed only with grief and hatred!'

'He will return before nightfall, when he comes to his senses and realises that he cannot conduct a meaningful search in the dark. Then you must lull him to sleep in your arms.'

'And if he does *not* return?' she challenged him as tears welled in her eyes. 'What if he succeeds in finding Dempsey, who must be desperate to avoid capture, while Edward is driven by nothing but the pain in his heart, and is slowed down through weariness?'

Francis took Elizabeth's hands in his and lowered his voice. 'May I confide in you? And if I do, will you make a solemn vow not to repeat what I have to tell you?'

16

Edward's plan was vindicated when their final prisoner was talked down from the roof cavity by Farnham. The man's name was Brother John Ignatius, and he was dressed as befitted a member of the Jesuit Order, in a plain black soutane, tied around which was a fading gold cincture. The man appeared to be in his early thirties and seemed none the worse for his days without food and drink. His face bore a serene expression, as if unaware of the peril he was in, and he asked only that he be allowed to wash. This request was granted, and he was offered food and drink, which he consumed sparingly despite what must have been intense hunger. Everyone who had dealings with him remarked on his kind, even saintly, appearance, and wondered at his composure and his seeming acceptance of his capture.

Partly because of that, and because they had exhausted all the places in Nether Hall in which men might be kept secure, Brother John was confined in a small chamber to the rear of the second floor, too high from the ground to permit his leaping from the window. But the elementary precautions could not be overlooked, so Poultney agreed to resume overall supervision of the basement in which were held the ruffians who had admitted to having been recruited by Dempsey, while Edward and Francis would take it in turns to guard the door of Brother John's chamber. They agreed between themselves that they would do so in four-hour shifts.

Two days later, Edward was pacing up and down the hallway outside the man's room when the door opened and Brother John appeared.

'You are out here, bored to distraction,' he said, smiling at Edward, 'while I am inside here, similarly afflicted. Why do you not join me inside, where we may converse? You have my word upon the blood of Christ that I will make no attempt to escape, and even if I do you are armed with a sword.'

Edward did as requested, and the two men sat facing each other in seats inside the window bay that overlooked what had once been a vegetable garden.

'You would shrink from drawing the blood of a man of God, I suspect,' Brother John suggested in a soft voice.

Edward was not to be beguiled into letting his guard slip. 'You mentioned the "Blood of Christ",' he said. 'Is that not the name of your secret brotherhood?'

Brother John maintained his somewhat patronising smile as he responded, 'All believers of the true faith are in some way united by the blood that Christ shed on the cross, in order to redeem all mankind.'

'Spare me the canting drivel,' Edward sneered. 'I was raised in an orphanage by so-called "holy brothers" of the so-called "true faith". I can still recall their daily gluttony while we children were fed barely enough to keep us alive. The wealth for that came from the donations of pious benefactors who were deceived into believing that they were doing God's work, when they were merely funding a sinful life for the hypocrites who were in charge of the orphanage. One could look out of the windows at night and see town prostitutes slipping away with the brothers' coins.'

Brother John sighed. 'It was because of such tales — many of them exaggerated — that the Antichrist Cromwell succeeded in closing so many holy houses. That, and the greed of his paymaster, Henry Tudor. It cannot be denied that mere men sometimes fall to temptations of the flesh, but that serves to test them and make saints of those who successfully resist.'

'So you regard yourself as a saint, do you?' Edward snarled bitterly. 'You, who are the inspiration for a gang of cut-throats led by a double-dyed villain who murdered my mother in cold blood?'

'God moves in mysterious ways, my son,' Brother John replied serenely.

Edward's temper was rapidly fraying. 'As far as I am concerned, he does not move in *any* way that a true man would wish to follow,' he spat back. 'Your version of the Church prevented my father and mother from enjoying a life together united by true love, simply because he was one of your kind — a hypocrite in a cassock. This caused my mother a lifetime of grief, and she was obliged to consign me to an orphanage until I attained my fifteenth year. It was quite by accident that my mother and I were reunited only last week, and then one of your disciples took her life in a callous act of wilful slaughter.'

Brother John's smile hardened slightly, but he replied in a soft voice. 'It is obvious that you have suffered greatly in a matter of the heart, my son, but if you offer up your suffering to Christ the Redeemer, he will hold you up in your darkest hour.'

'Don't preach God to me!' Edward shouted. 'The only one holding me up in my darkest hour is my beautiful wife, who is worth more to me than all your mealy-mouthed preaching and your plaster saints! When they have you on the rack in the Tower of London, you can call in vain for your God! I hope you suffer the torments of Hell for what you have brought about in this place!'

Without any conscious thought, his hand had come to rest on his sword hilt. If Brother John was intimidated by this, it didn't show in his face, which still bore a patient, almost pitying, smile.

At that moment the door opened and Francis appeared in the doorway. He looked meaningfully at Edward's sword hand before commenting, 'Not before time, it would seem. It would not be good for your soul to kill a priest, but more importantly Burghley has arrived with reinforcements and wishes to meet us in the great hall. He has already spoken with Marlowe, and he is not best pleased.'

Baron Burghley was certainly not in a jovial mood as he waved Edward and Francis into the downstairs hall, where Poultney was already seated with a face that looked as if it had recently been slapped. Through gritted teeth the recently arrived Burghley congratulated them on having secured so many prisoners, and having disrupted the activities inside Nether Hall. Then he fell silent, as if challenging someone to say something. Francis and Edward played their familiar game with their eyes, each challenging the other, and eventually it was Edward who weakened.

'At least I will not be required to play the part of some shepherd turned warrior king in that turgid masque by Marlowe,' he observed.

Burghley's face went dark red as he replied, 'It was necessary to release Marlowe from your custody with a cringing apology for his unjustified detention.'

It fell silent again, and this time it was Francis who braved the storm.

'We did him no injury, and when he insisted that he had the protection of Her Majesty we allowed him the degree of comfort and courtesy appropriate for one suspected of being involved in a treasonous conspiracy. Was he speaking truth when he claimed the immunity of royal favour?'

'He was not working for Her Majesty directly,' Burghley explained. 'I was not aware that he was, like yourselves, engaged in covert enquiries regarding what was going on here. But he had Walsingham's seal.'

'What is that?' Edward asked, since it seemed to be expected of someone.

Burghley sighed. 'Francis Walsingham, until his untimely but merciful death last year, was the co-ordinator of my group of covert investigators into Catholic intrigues in this country. He was a tried and trusted sniffer-out of conspirators, and he employed many men in the unearthing of those sent by Rome to undermine Elizabeth's rule. Walsingham brought about the undoing of the Scots Mary and the revelation of the Babington Plot, and most recently he worked directly under me in smoking out Jesuits sent from the seminaries across the Channel to undermine the throne and to promote secret pockets of Catholic resistance. In this work he made use of lesser men well placed to worm their way into the confidences of others, and to each of them he gave a likeness of his seal, forged from a common silver cast, for when they, like Marlowe, found themselves under arrest. This was an obvious risk when engaging in subterfuge. When your man rode into London, he was bearing one of these which had been produced by Marlowe.'

'So you have been obliged to release him?' Francis asked.

Burghley nodded grimly. 'Indeed I have. He was furious that I had ordered that this place be infiltrated when, in his opinion, he had already undertaken that mission successfully. He knew of Walsingham's death, but was by then too hot on the trail of traitors to abandon his work.'

'So while we were conducting covert enquiries into what was going on here at Nether Hall on your instruction, Marlowe was doing likewise at the behest of Walsingham?' Edward summarised.

'That would indeed appear to be the case,' Burghley conceded with bad grace, 'but the result of your joint efforts is the capture of one who has been a thorn in the side of the English court for some time. I speak of the man who calls himself "Brother John Ignatius".'

'Had I not intervened when I did,' Francis said, glancing at Edward, 'he would now be the *late* Brother John Ignatius.'

'He may well acquire that status when Master Topcliffe has done with him,' said Burghley grimly. 'Before you ask, Topcliffe is the queen's trusted interrogator inside the Tower, where the so-called "Brother John" will be taken under his real name of Robert Southwell.'

'I recall that name from a previous meeting,' Edward replied.

'We believe him to be the man behind "The Brotherhood of the Blood of Christ", and a leading light in the smuggling of Jesuit priests into Catholic houses here in England,' Burghley explained. 'Depending on his capacity to withstand some of the more refined instruments of persuasion employed by Master Topcliffe, he may well facilitate the disbanding of the entire network.'

'So our work has not been either in vain, or a superfluous addition to the work of Master Marlowe?' Edward offered in an effort to lighten the atmosphere.

'That has to be conceded, and I am obliged to advise you that Marlowe did not see through your disguise,' said Burghley. 'Had he done so, you and he might have worked more closely together. He also added that he lost a fine and promising actor when you unwisely broke your cover in order to prevent Master Barton from being assassinated by those oafs currently being held in the cellar.'

'So Master Marlowe has been released, and this Robert Southwell is to be taken back to the Tower,' Poultney summarised. 'What of the others?'

'They go to the Tower,' Burghley advised him tersely. 'We shall put each of them to the question. I have no doubt that they will, between them, give us much more information regarding the plans that were being hatched to meet up at Chatsworth and form an army that would march on London under the banner of Arbella Stuart. We may even be advised of how much she knew of what was being planned in her name.'

'We also need confessions regarding the murders of the two justices,' Edward reminded him.

Not to be outdone, Francis added, 'And the murders of a Nottingham prostitute and an escaped prisoner, which we believe were committed in order to cover up their presence at a house in Cotgrave.'

'We shall see what we shall see,' Burghley replied as he waved his hand to signal that the brief meeting was over. 'You gentlemen may resume your bailiff duties in your respective jurisdictions, while I will journey south with the enlarged Tower party and all our prisoners. I am adding Sir Ralph Farnham to the list, although I suspect that someone in high office in London will wheedle him a pardon on the grounds that he is a feeble old fool who is not long for this life anyway. I shall write to advise you of how matters progress, and my thanks for your loyal service to Her Majesty.'

Later that day, both bailiffs and Elizabeth mounted their horses and trotted north through the village of Sutton Bonington on their way home.

'I suppose we should be grateful that we came out of all this with our lives,' Francis muttered. 'And you got to meet your mother, Edward,' he added, to a loud expression of displeasure from Elizabeth.

Edward smiled and reached across his saddle to grasp her hand. 'You need not fear that the mere mention of her name will cause me to become overwrought. But you should both accept that once we have settled back into our humdrum existence, I shall go in search of Dempsey. Perhaps Burghley will be able to reveal his whereabouts.'

Francis and Elizabeth said nothing, but exchanged meaningful glances. Then, as the church spires of St Mary's and St Nicholas's churches became visible across the river plain of the silvery Trent, the conversation reverted to what might await each of them upon their return to regular duties. For Francis it was a spate of burglaries in the wealthier houses of the town, while Edward needed to travel north to Papplewick to investigate a case of sheep rustling on the fringes of Sherwood Forest. He discharged this duty while Elizabeth made her way back to Thurland Hall.

A few hours later, Edward returned from Papplewick with a local farm labourer tied to the back of his horse, who he threw into the Shire Hall dungeons. When he arrived home, he was advised by Elizabeth that Burghley had journeyed back north and wished to meet with Edward on his return.

Not bothering to change out of his riding clothes, Edward lost no time in striding across the courtyard of Thurland Hall and into the great hall, where Burghley was seated by the fire, clutching a mug of mulled ale. Sir John Holles looked up as Edward entered and beckoned him over.

'It is good that you returned when you did, since Baron Burghley has orders to travel north as soon as he has concluded his business here.'

'Chatsworth?' Edward enquired.

'That is *not* part of my business here,' Burghley advised. 'First, I must advise you that those oafs who were led — if that is quite the appropriate term — by Dempsey gave us the information we wanted when faced with the addition of a few inches to their height on the rack. There can be no doubt that armed bands were being assembled across the nation under the banner of "The Brotherhood of the Blood of Christ". They freely admitted to the murders of the two royal justices, the town prostitute and the escaped prisoner. If anything, they seemed proud of their achievements.'

'So the network has been broken up?' Edward asked.

Burghley nodded. 'Soldiers from the Tower have been sent to various parts of the nation, and she who was alleged to have inspired the uprising is being summoned to court to explain what, if anything, she knew about it. Marlowe is back among the low taverns of Cheapside, peddling his drivel, while Sir Ralph Farnham is living under the furlough of a cousin in Southwark, who will be a thousand marks poorer if Farnham misbehaves again. His estate is forfeit, and currently open to bids.'

'That is a considerable amount of information,' Edward said, struggling to take it all in.

'There is more. I have a message from Her Majesty, which is basically her heartfelt thanks for your labours on her behalf. I have already conveyed those sentiments to your colleague Master Barton, who has received a monetary reward directly from her that should keep him well supplied with ladies of easy virtue until well into the New Year.'

'I, on the other hand, have a wife and a house that has just been completed,' said Edward mischievously. 'Did Her Majesty send bed linen?'

'Guard your tongue, young man, if you wish to enjoy what she *did* send,' Burghley replied with a frown that denoted an end to any remaining levity. 'Strangely enough she remembered that you were recently married, and was most impressed by what I told her regarding your good lady's contribution to the unmasking of the Brotherhood. She is anxious that you should both share in her bounty, and entrusted me with the task of identifying how that might best be achieved. Sir John told me of your new house being ready for occupation, and today I visited several establishments here in town that supply furnishings, carpets, curtains and assorted linen. Each of them has been commissioned to supply whatever you require for your new home, and the accounts are to be directed to Westminster for my personal attention.'

'You are most generous,' Edward stammered.

'Not I, but Her Majesty,' Burghley replied. 'But if there is ought else I can assist you with, then you may ask. I do not promise that I will comply, but you may ask.'

'There *is* one thing,' Edward replied as his face clouded. 'Is there any intelligence regarding the whereabouts of that evil dog Dempsey?'

Edward, Elizabeth and Francis stood watching the carts being unloaded, and all manner of furnishings and drapes being carried inside the newly completed house by youths employed for the day by the merchants. Francis was as excited by the prospect of having his best friends living across the road from him as Edward and Elizabeth were about their imminent transfer from Thurland Hall into their new home.

'It's good to see so many local tradesmen benefitting from Her Majesty's largesse,' Francis commented.

Edward looked sideways at him with a lewd grin. 'Other local traders will benefit considerably from the money that she gave you, but the trade in question is one that we would ordinarily prosecute.'

'I will ignore that slur upon my character on this joyous occasion,' Francis replied. 'When may I anticipate being invited to a fine dinner to celebrate your new home?'

'As soon as I've tracked down Dempsey and taken him to Leicester Gaol charged with murder,' Edward replied grimly. 'Elizabeth and I have agreed that the death of the man who murdered my mother must come first, if I am to settle into our new home with an easy mind.'

Elizabeth kicked Francis's ankle. 'I believe that Francis has something to tell you,' she said pointedly.

Edward laughed. 'If it is regarding the first stew in which Her Majesty's money will be redistributed, and it lies in the county, then he may rely on my instructing my constables to walk straight past during their regular tours of such places.'

'It's not that, Edward,' Francis began as his face set in anticipation. 'You must promise, first of all, that what I am about to tell you will be investigated by you no further.'

'How can you expect me to turn my back on *two* breaches of the law I am sworn to uphold?'

'This second breach was in Leicestershire.'

It fell chillingly silent as Elizabeth reached out to grip Edward's hand.

'Why would I have any ongoing interest in a crime committed in Leicestershire, unless it is to do with my mother's murder?'

'It is,' Francis admitted glumly, 'and it has a direct bearing on when you may make plans to become my neighbour.'

'Please spare me the riddles, Francis,' Edward replied in irritation. 'To what are you referring?'

'Dempsey is already dead.'

Elizabeth gripped Edward's hand even harder as he grasped the implications of what he was being told. After a lengthy silence, he asked, 'How do you know this?'

'I cannot answer that question directly without your being obliged, by your oath of office, to pass on what I tell you to the Sheriff of Leicestershire. I will only give you my solemn word that Dempsey is dead. This means that you are free to set about the occupation of your new home.'

'Why did you not tell me this much sooner, since you know only too well how it has dominated my every waking thought since my mother's death?'

'We did not wish to distract you from certain other important matters,' was all Francis could offer by way of explanation.

Edward turned to stare at Elizabeth. 'We?' he echoed. 'How could you have known that Francis was keeping this vital intelligence from me and not share it with me, in order to lessen my anger and grief?'

'Forgive me, my sweet,' Elizabeth pleaded, 'but he swore me to an oath of secrecy.'

'Secrecy from your own husband? Is this how you intend to conduct our marriage, by keeping from me things of which I should be aware?'

'I believe that I am required back across the road in my own house,' Francis announced diplomatically. 'And since your wife chose this moment to disclose that I was keeping something from you, let me advise you before I depart that *she* has something to tell *you*. And so I bid the happy couple a good day.'

'What is this?' Edward demanded as he turned to face Elizabeth with raised eyebrows. 'Am I being made a fool by those dearest to me?'

'The time was not right until this moment,' Elizabeth assured him. 'Had Francis not confided in me that you had no need to seek out that dreadful Dempsey in order to bring him to justice, I would have told you earlier, because then it would not have been wise for you to leave us both alone.'

'Us?' Edward queried again. 'Francis is more than capable of looking after both himself and you. Who *else* would I have been abandoning?'

Elizabeth leaned forward and kissed him warmly on the lips. 'While we were down in Mountsorrel, another miracle occurred. While you were finding a mother, you were also creating her first grandchild.'

When his mouth dropped open in surprise, she closed it gently with her finger, then stepped backwards to wave in the direction of the new house.

'We must lose no time in creating our own hearth, Edward. I am with child.'

A NOTE TO THE READER

Dear Reader,

Thank you for taking the time to read this second novel in the series about Edward Mountsorrel and his life as bailiff to the Sheriff of Nottinghamshire. In the first, *The Castle Abductions*, he met Elizabeth Porter while helping to rescue a group of women abducted from his adopted town, and in this second novel he spends time in the county of his birth, seeking to keep the nation safe from any uprising.

The year in which this was set — 1591 — was one of considerable uncertainty for those who were tasked with guarding and advising the long-reigning Elizabeth I. The Spanish Armada had been blown off course by the winds of misfortune, but the Pope and his ardent followers in the Catholic nations across the Channel had not abandoned the prospect of welcoming England back into the bosom of Rome.

Elizabeth was now almost sixty years of age, and no-one could have anticipated that she would remain on the English throne for another twelve years. But it was obvious that she could no longer expect to bear any natural heir, even had she deigned to take a husband. There was therefore much speculation around the English court regarding her successor. If the bloodlines were followed, then there were two candidates of approximately equal standing, thanks to the marital history of Elizabeth's Aunt Margaret.

Margaret Tudor, the older sister of Henry VIII, had first married James IV of Scotland, and her granddaughter by that marriage had been Mary Stuart, Queen of Scotland, whose threat to the English Crown had been ended by an executioner in Fotheringhay Castle four years previously. But Mary had left a son, James, by her marriage to Lord Darnley, and he now ruled Scotland as James VI. He was avowedly Protestant, and many regarded him as the obvious heir to Elizabeth, in direct line as the great-grandson of the Tudor progenitor Henry VII.

James's claim was reinforced by the fact that Margaret Tudor had remarried following the death of James IV, and her daughter by that second marriage, to the Earl of Angus, was Lady Margaret Douglas, the mother of Lord Darnley. James of Scotland therefore had a second claim to the throne, through the same line, in the same degree, through the two different marriages of Margaret Tudor.

But his was not the only claim through this second line, because Lord Darnley had a younger brother, Charles, who married Elizabeth Cavendish, the daughter of the woman of the same name who is better known to history as 'Bess of Hardwick'. Their daughter, Arbella Stuart, could therefore claim Margaret Tudor as her great-grandmother, and Henry VII as her great-great-grandfather. She was a devout Catholic, and following the death of her aunt Mary, Queen of Scots, the hopes of English Catholics centred on the possibility that she would became Queen Arbella. Whichever way it went, the Tudor line would be replaced by the Stuarts, but Elizabeth was stubbornly silent on the matter of naming an heir.

However, Rome had not abandoned its interference in English politics, despite the failure of its head-on attack via the Armada it had blessed. Elizabeth had been excommunicated, and her English subjects had been openly encouraged to rebel against her rule. In addition, the Catholic Church had partly financed a network of seminaries on the European mainland that were designated 'English Colleges', and were training priests to cross the Channel in secret in order to keep the flame of the 'true faith' burning.

This was the era in which English spies under Baron Burghley and Francis Walsingham were smoking out Jesuit priests who were being welcomed into, and hidden inside, English manor houses whose owners still practised Catholicism. Many an old English manor house still has its 'priest hole' in which the Jesuit guest could be hidden from view when Walsingham's 'pursuivants' came calling. More than one ghost story has as its origin the fate that befell those who were caught, or perished inside a secret chamber built into the Tudor edifice.

This is an era of English history ripe with low-hanging fruit for the historical novelist, and I filled my basket when writing this novel, dreaming up main characters such as Edward and Elizabeth Mountsorrel and Francis Barton, and calling on real characters from history to play their parts. Baron Burghley could clearly not be ignored, as he continued to employ the spy network established by the recently deceased Francis Walsingham. One of his greatest quarries was the Jesuit Robert Southwell, who features in this novel. Southwell was eventually caught, tortured in the Tower and hanged, drawn and quartered at Tyburn as a Catholic traitor. Almost four hundred years later, in 1970, he was canonised as *Saint* Robert Southwell.

I also could not resist employing one of the period's most enigmatic characters, Christopher Marlowe. Those who have heard of him will know him as one of the first Elizabethan playwrights, and scholars of English Literature have argued for years over whether or not he wrote the works attributed to Shakespeare. Historians have also crossed swords on Marlowe's precise non-literary role in those uneasy years during which Catholic rebels were suspected of lurking under every bed, and what little is known of his life only serves to feed the mystery. He disappeared from public view during his final year at Cambridge University, but when the masters of his college baulked at awarding him his master's degree, they were overruled by the Privy Council on the curiously worded grounds that he had been engaged in 'matters touching the benefit of his country'. These matters are thought to have been his enrolment in one of the English Colleges abroad that were training Jesuits, in order to spy on their activities and report back to his paymasters at court.

Although he regularly described himself as an atheist, he is also believed to have been regarded by his contemporaries as a closet Catholic, and some historians also credit him with having been employed as a tutor to Arbella Stuart under the assumed name of "Morley". There was enough mystery to tempt any historical novelist such as myself, and one of his greatest works, *Tamburlaine*, had been published by the year in which this novel was set, and did indeed call for a powerful martial orator to carry off the lead role.

I was delighted to be able to employ, as settings for the latter half of the novel, the quaint Leicestershire villages of Quorndon (now known simply as 'Quorn') and Mountsorrel. They remain today much as they must have looked in 1591, and afford the modern tourist a delightful day out, or an overnight stay among some of the most verdant and fruitful countryside in the English Midlands. Alas Nottingham, where Edward and Francis are based, has changed beyond recognition, and the echoes of horses' hooves on narrow cobbled streets have been replaced by the relentless drumming of heavy commercial tyres on the asphalt of contemporary city thoroughfares.

I genuinely hope that this novel provided a few hours of pleasant diversion and a convincing step back in time. As ever, I would be delighted to see a review of it posted on **Amazon** or **Goodreads**. Alternatively, feel free to visit, and contact me on, my author website: **davidfieldauthor.com**.

Happy reading!

David

Sapere Books is an exciting new publisher of brilliant fiction and popular history.

To find out more about our latest releases and our monthly bargain books visit our website:
saperebooks.com

Printed in Great Britain
by Amazon

63359541R00111